For Maria

The Moon Stealers & The Quest for the Silver Bough

TIM FLANAGAN

Copyright © 2012 Tim Flanagan

All rights reserved.

ISBN: 1478136707
ISBN-13: 978-1478136705

CONTENTS

	Acknowledgments	i
1	The Graveyard	1
2	Inside MI6	5
3	A Call to Duty	10
4	The Secret Meeting	15
5	The Statue of Saint Vitus	18
6	Newton Rise Abattoir	24
7	London to York	27
8	A Birds Eye View	31
9	The Night Watchman	36
10	The Faerie Ring	39
11	The League of White Knights	43
12	The Box of Rocks	47
13	Proof of Identity	50
14	A Gruesome Discovery	55
15	Unlocking the Key	58
16	Sir Hadwyn's Inscription	63
17	The Theft	68
18	The Escape Tunnel	73
19	A Restless Knight	79
20	The Pathology Report	83
21	St Giles' Cathedral	87
22	Edgar Tells the Truth	91
23	Bacteria on the Move	95
24	Edinburgh Central Library	98
25	A Shocking Revelation	102
26	The Silver Bough	108
27	Attack on Parsley Bottom	114
28	Running into Danger	117
29	Bishops Green Station	122
30	Rosery Wood	126
31	The Ice House	130
32	One Way Out	136
33	The Magic Portal	141
34	Escape to Butterwick Hall	145
35	A Message from Afar	149

The Everlasting Night

A darkened veil upon the virgin Earth,
A seed for consumption gives rise to birth.
The wind of change is quick to bite,
And so begins the everlasting night.

Before the reign of man does close,
Faith will lie between old foes.
But Faerie help is far from sight,
A growing everlasting night.

From the shadow a hope emerges,
To bind, and in the night to join us.
A growing grain of pure white light,
To clear the everlasting night.

For dawn to come, a sun must rise,
To burn the cloud and scorch their eyes.
Unite together for England's plight,
To cease the everlasting night.

ACKNOWLEDGMENTS

Many people helped in the writing in this book. Thanks to all my brutally honest proof readers and those that advised in the development of the story line, including Mark Wilkinson, Chloe Keenan, Bryan Cooper, Margaret Flanagan and Scarlett Thomas. Special thanks to my son, James, who read, then re-read every chapter as I wrote them and for helping with the original idea of the Moon Stealers. Thanks also to my dad, Roger, who gave advice about the police and forensic details.

The biggest thanks need to go to my wife, Maria, who graciously allows me time to lock myself away in my cupboard under the stairs and write whilst she occupies the children.

Thanks also to you, the reader. Without your support writing becomes a lonely business, so I hope you enjoy the story and join me on other uncharted adventures in the future.

1 THE GRAVEYARD

It all begins with Peter Crisp...

It was deadly quiet in Parsley Bottom graveyard and very, very dark. The reassuring light from the street lamps did not reach this part of the usually peaceful village; instead everything looked like a scene from an old black and white film, the stones and shapes picked out by the white glow from the moon. Cracked and crumbling gravestones stuck out of the ground, unattended after so many years of neglect, surrounded by clumps of long grass and the skeletal remains of bunches of flowers long forgotten. The rusty gate clung to the old stone wall by just one hinge, leaning on the dirt for support, unable to make a sound. Even the bats, which had been known to put on quite a show for the locals in the past, had hidden themselves beneath the eaves of the church roof and tucked their heads inside their leathery wings, knowing what evil was stirring amongst the gravestones below. Tonight, Parsley Bottom graveyard was not the place to be; unless you were already dead of course.

Peter Crisp lay on a blanket behind one of the larger gravestones not too far from the stone wall on the west side of the old decaying church, shielding himself from the cool air that seeped off the river at the bottom of the graveyard and across the ground. Because the night sky was so clear tonight there was a late spring frost which had already started to make the grass around him crisp and stiff. The white stones began to shimmer magically as small crystals of water froze into dustings of ice and glimmered in the moonlight.

'One night,' he thought to himself, 'that's all I have to do.' He tried to convince himself that it would be easy and that he would be fine as he nervously hugged the sleeping bag tight against him and pulled it high up beneath his chin.

'One night,' he said to himself again. Hearing his voice inside his head reassured Peter that he was not alone. But, Peter had never been alone, not truly.

He pulled his hand up so that he could just peep at his wrist watch without letting out any of the heat he had accumulated inside the sleeping bag so he could see what time the luminous clock face said.

Twenty eight minutes past midnight.

The sun would be starting to come up at some point within the next six hours and he would have proved to everyone at school that he was as brave and tough as Jimmy Cox, not to mention winning Jimmy's new skateboard in the process. If he didn't manage it and went home early, he would remain the school weirdo that no one wanted to know. This was the dare of all dares; stay in the graveyard for one night.

Peter wasn't what you would call a popular twelve year old boy. His mother could never keep up with his growth and as a consequence his clothes always appeared to be two sizes too small. His thick brown hair grew too quick for his head and often his fringe would cover his spectacles making him feel that he was constantly looking out of a window with the curtains half drawn. Peter was different to all of the other children at school, he could see things that they couldn't, which often made them stare at him or call him names. On the brighter side; he could run fast. The other kids at school would often be impressed with the speed he could run, until his long uncoordinated legs caused him to trip over his own feet. Then they would laugh at him and mock the way his legs got tangled up amongst themselves. Jimmy, by contrast, was popular. He lived in a pub with his parents, was good at sports and always had clothes that fitted. In fact some of them weren't even strictly part of the school uniform, but Jimmy always seemed to be able to get away with it.

'It's just like camping.' Peter told himself, trying to keep positive. That afternoon he had collected a few items from home to bring with him and help him through the night. To occupy his mind he mentally went through his list for the twenty third time, just to make sure he had everything:

A torch
Blanket and sleeping bag
Thick coat and hat
Chocolate Bar
Can of Fizzy Orange

Peter squeezed his left arm reassuringly against his chest, making sure that Dudley, his favourite bear, was still there. He would never admit to owning a teddy bear at his age, but Dudley had been a favourite of his since he was one year old.

C-r-a-a-c-k !

The sound of a sharp snap echoed around the graveyard. It suddenly made Peter forget about his list and remind him exactly where he was. Instinctively he sat upright and twisted to look towards where the sound came from. He stopped breathing and started to shiver, the sleeping bag had slipped slightly down around his shoulders.

He waited for another sound, but nothing happened. It felt like ages until the silence of the graveyard returned and he began to relax slightly again.

'Probably just squirrels or hedgehogs moving about in the bushes looking for food. That's all it was,' he said to himself trying to convince himself that the sound was nothing to worry about as he lay himself back down.

He decided to cough loudly to scare any small animals away then waited again. No other sounds disturbed the night air so he pulled his sleeping bag closer to him once again, pulled the zip up as high as he could, closed his eyes and squeezed Dudley against his chest. To stop himself from hearing other noises he began to hum a nameless tune to himself until he slowly drifted into sleep.

The arrival of the bright moon within the starry night sky had, unknown to Peter, begun to wake up another occupant of the graveyard, one that did not like the brightness of the sun but preferred the black cloak of night to do its hunting.

At first you wouldn't even have known they were there, but as they moved out from the shadows of the stones, two hooded shapes slid slowly across the muddy grass. Their movement was so slow and smooth that they could have been traveling on wheels or skating across a frozen lake.

They were heading in the direction of Peter.

Peter was sleeping lightly, his ears unknowingly tuned into the sounds of the graveyard. Occasionally, he heard the rustling sound of the wind as it blew through the leaves on the trees or a gentle splash from the shallow river, all of which he subconsciously accepted and ignored. But there was another sound now, one he was unfamiliar with that made him open his eyes. He lifted his head above the gravestone and looked around. Everything was black except for the shine of the moon reflecting off the cold white surface of the gravestones, just as it had been the last time he had looked. But something was different and he couldn't quite tell what it was. To start with he could hear a sound that seemed to be out of place; a sound that reminded Peter of thick gravy bubbling in a pan ready for a Sunday dinner. There was also a strange smell like a piece of mouldy bread that had been left in its bag for too long to go damp and furry.

He took the torch out from the bottom of his sleeping bag, turned it on and swung the light around him like a beam from a lighthouse. It all looked normal, although the noise had now stopped. Reassured that everything was alright, he switched the light off and snuggled back down inside the sleeping bag.

After a few seconds Peter thought that he could hear the thick bubbling sound again, but this time it seemed to be nearer to him; so close in fact that it almost sounded like it was coming from the direction somewhere towards the end of his sleeping bag where his feet were.

'I don't scare that easily Jimmy,' Peter shouted mockingly into the night, his voice echoing in the night air. 'You need to try harder than that if you want me to go home early.' Peter thought it was probably Jimmy or one of his friends trying to scare him, but he wasn't going to be put off that easy. He switched the torch on again and placed it on the grass beside him so that the beam was shining towards his feet.

Once again Peter settled down inside the warm sleeping bag and closed his eyes. He didn't know if there was enough power in the torch batteries to last through the night, but he was sure that Jimmy would soon get bored and go home. After that, Peter didn't remember much, he drifted comfortably back into his light sleep in the hope that the next time he opened his eyes the sun would be starting to come out.

The hooded shapes waited before warily moving closer towards Peter. In the middle of the night most people were fast asleep and could do nothing to help him. His screams and cries quickly became muffled by an unknown killer until all that was left was a blanket and sleeping bag tangled together in a heap behind a gravestone.

2. INSIDE MI6

It felt like most of the past two years that Steven Knight had been working for the British Government, had involved nothing but sitting behind a desk writing reports for senior officials. But, unknown to Steven, today was going to be different. He entered, as normal, through the high security checkpoints inside London's MI6 headquarters and stepped into the highly polished glass elevator to take him up to the seventh floor where his desk was awaiting him, along with the pile of paperwork that he had left there the night before.

From the seating area in the atrium of the building, where many suited men whispered selective truths into the ears of their colleagues, a tall man dashed across towards the lift just as the doors were about to slide shut. As Steven reached for the button to hold the doors open, the man athletically slid his tall frame through the narrow gap, nodded good morning to him and stood looking out of the glass lift as it began to move smoothly up.

Steven thought that he recognised most people in the building, but not this man. And his appearance was not one you could forget in a hurry. His height was the first striking thing about him; by comparing him with his own height, Steven judged him to be around seven foot tall. His black hair hung in dreadlocks to his shoulders and he obviously kept himself fit as Steven could make out the curves of the shoulder and back muscles beneath the man's tailored dark blue pin striped suit. But the most unusual thing about this man was the silvery white scar that cut deeply into his black skin from below one eye to his jaw line.

After a few seconds the elevator stopped at the fourth floor and another man entered.

'Morning Knight,' said a handsome man to Steven. 'Have you caught any aliens yet?' he continued with a mocking smile on his face.

'Not yet Davison,' replied Steven. Despite trying to look comfortable with the jape, he knew that he was the butt of all jokes within the building, together with the rest of the department he worked in.

'Actually, I was going to come and talk to you,' continued Davison trying to be charming and sincere. 'Something strange happened to me this morning at breakfast. Just as I was about to take the last mouth full of cereal from the bowl, it looked like it had arranged itself into letters that spelt out a word.'

'Really?' asked Steven, slightly warily, waiting for the punch line.

'I wrote it down so I wouldn't forget,' Davison pulled a notepad out of his inside pocket and thumbed through it. 'Here we go; it spelt out the word ANILE. Strange, eh? Anyway,' he paused, 'I thought you should know.'

'Thanks,' nodded Steven trying to work out if Davison was being serious or not, 'I'll look out for any other cereal related reports and let you know.'

Desperately trying to stop himself from laughing, Davison turned his face down towards his feet, his lips tightly clamped together not wanting to betray his joke.

'Here's my stop,' said Davison as an electronic bell chimed the arrival to the sixth floor and the doors began to open. 'I've got some real foreign threats to catch. Bye.' He enthusiastically jumped out of the elevator and disappeared from view, but as the doors closed, Steven was sure that he heard Davison burst into laughter from further along the corridor.

As the elevator hummed into action once again the tall man continued to look out of the glass as if he were on his own. At the next floor Steven stepped forward to get out and glanced back towards him. For a split second he thought that the tall man was using the reflection in the glass to discreetly assess and observe Steven, but he could be doing nothing more than simply looking out of the glass. Steven felt an uncomfortable shiver work its way down his back and was glad to hear the doors close behind him as he walked down the long corridor towards his office.

Steven was a member of the Unexplained Foreign Activity Department (UFA) a lesser known section of MI6, Britain's Secret Intelligence Service. During 1950, in the aftermath of panic caused by Orson Welles' War of the World's as well as supposed real alien sightings like the Roswell Incident in America, the Prime Minister at the time, Clement Attlee, commissioned UFA. Since World War II, he considered Britain's security to be at risk not only from other countries, but also from other life forms.

But so far, no alternative life forms had ever been found.

Or as the conspiracy theorists would say, none that had been officially reported.

To date the most interesting things that had landed on Steven's desk included reports of strange activity in a laptop in Appletreewick, North Yorkshire, a possessed Caretaker at a School in Piddle River, Dorset and a Hamster called Nibbles that was thought to be 452 years old in Tutts Clump,

Berkshire. It seemed that all Steven had done so far was investigate hoaxes. Never once had he felt like there was any possible shred of genuine alien activity in Britain, or ever likely to be.

Recently, Steven had been wondering whether this was the right job for him. The team he worked for was the joke of the whole building, nothing ever happened and it was amazing that it continued to get funding. Many rumours circulated the office about the source of the funding; the official explanation was that the government paid for all departments in MI6 including the UFA, but the most recent rumour doing the rounds was that a private drugs company now supplemented the government to continue the UFA. Whatever the reason Steven was considering a transfer to another department with a bit more excitement like Counter Terrorism that Davison worked in.

Ever since Steven was eight years old he had believed that there must be something else out there and he wanted to be at the front when it was discovered. Probably the biggest reason for his motivation was simply the fact that he was endlessly searching for his parents who had mysteriously disappeared in the Forest of Dean. To this day he still kept the newspaper cuttings about his parent's disappearance inside an old scrap book, the paper yellow now with age and going soft along the well thumbed edges.

Steven approached an office door with the words 'Unexplained Foreign Activity Department – UFA' etched in the glass. He swiped his security card through the electronic reader and waited for the click of the lock to disengage before pushing the door open. Once through, he walked to his cubicle, a small area enclosed on three sides by a thin partition to the other cubicles that joined onto his. His small desk was overloaded with books on conspiracy theories, and brown cardboard folders stuffed with paper and stacked in a pile that had overflowed across his computer keyboard.

He shared the office with three other people; Jake, a fat balding single man who thrived on conspiracy theories and regularly updated a blog which officials at Whitehall naturally monitored and censored when necessary, giving fuel to Jake's obsessions. Gwen, a divorced woman who seemed to have one mission in life and that was to disprove any possible signs of alien life and on the way, cut men down at every opportunity just for her own amusement. Definitely an aggressive non believer. The fourth member of the team was Sir Adam Brooks, the official long suffering Head of the UFA. He had worked in the department for longer than Steven had been alive and, although decorated with a Knighthood, continued to be the object of many a joke within MI6, even amongst other senior members of staff. Unlike many of the other MI6 Heads of Department Sir Adam didn't carry an aura of power and authority with him, which is why Steven liked him. But it also made him feel sad; could he end up like Sir Adam, endlessly searching?

While he waited for the computer to warm up he scribbled the word ANILE on his note pad. He had been thinking about what Davison had said in the elevator, and as he looked at the word, he realised that if he rearranged the letters it could also spell ALIEN, so it was probably just Davison's idea of a joke.

He picked up the folder he had left at the top of the pile the night before and slid the top sheet out. It was the latest hoax that he had been given to investigate. He had received a memo from a local police station in the small town of Wettyfoot in Scotland, where a local resident had reported seeing Lock Ness monster babies in his garden pond. Steven was waiting for a full report from the police at Wettyfoot, but a sample of the water and a dead baby monster had already been delivered to him.

Steven had already sent the sample of water, which was dark green with algae and as thick as custard, to the in-house laboratory for analysis and started researching all of the logical possibilities on the internet.

Although the creature had six lips and warty skin, it seemed that the most likely candidate for such a monster was a 4inch long worm called a Nematode and not anything extra terrestrial at all.

As soon as he received the official reports and analysis he could put the file away in the temperature controlled storage facility kept in the ground directly beneath the MI6 building and move on to the next wild goose chase.

'Good morning Steven,' said a clear and well spoken voice approaching the cubicles.

'Morning Sir Adam,' Steven instinctively replied as he stood up so that he could see over the partitions surrounding the cubicle.

'Good to see you're in early as usual. I wonder if you would come with me, I have something I need to discuss with you.'

'Of course Sir,' Steven agreed.

'Better leave those here,' Sir Adam indicated to the notepad and pencil Steven had just picked up off his desk. He turned around and began walking in the other direction, away from his own desk.

Steven struggled to keep up with his boss, even though he was about 40 years younger. What was a normal walking pace for Sir Adam was a breathless gallop for Steven.

'Can I ask what this is about?'

'Probably best not to. Not yet, at least,' replied Sir Adam vaguely.

Neither of them spoke any further as Sir Adam led Steven through an endless series of corridors and security doors that Steven was sure were in another part of the building that wouldn't normally be accessible, especially to staff of his lowly rank. He even wondered if they were in a totally different building altogether. He had heard rumours that there were tunnels and passageways under London's streets that lead to other government buildings to provide easy access for the Prime Minister and other senior members of the government to move quickly around London, especially during times of crisis, without anyone knowing.

One of the corridors turned sharply to the left and as they turned the corner Sir Adam placed a firm hand on Steven's chest preventing him from walking any further.

'A word of warning Steven,' Sir Adam whispered with a nervous look upon his face, 'do not trust everything and everyone you are about to meet. What you are about to see is only half the story. There are things they won't tell you.'

'What do you mean?'

Sir Adam looked around him nervously. 'I can't say any more. We are standing in a camera blind spot. We must keep walking, our movements are being monitored. If we don't walk seamlessly round the next corner, they will know we have delayed.'

Before Steven could ask any more questions, Sir Adam had taken a step round the corner leaving Steven no choice but to follow, even though he was now more confused than ever. At the end of the corridor he noticed the glowing single red eye of the camera watching as they approached what looked like a metal door.

To the right of the door was a card and retina scanner which Sir Adam automatically leant his head down to. After a few seconds the thick bolts inside the door frame clicked and a green light shone permitting access. The door swung slowly and heavily outwards towards them, revealing a small white washed room with no colour or decoration on the walls just a sterile metal conference table in the centre. Two people were already sitting at the desk with their backs to them. Steven reluctantly took a step inside the room followed by Sir Adam and the door closed silently behind them.

One of the men stood up and turned to face Steven, it was the tall scar faced man from the elevator.

3. A CALL TO DUTY

Joe Allen lay awake on top of his second hand mattress that sagged slightly in the middle, looking up at the ceiling. There had been an early morning knock on the front door to their small two bed roomed terrace house that had woken him up. He had heard his dad's tired feet making their way down the stairs to answer and now he could hear the deep voices of two men talking from the kitchen below. Joe turned and looked at his alarm clock, wondering whether to get up or not, but decided to stay where he was for a bit longer, despite the springs in the mattress digging into his back. He then heard movement from the room next to his; his grandmother must have heard the door knocking too. He listened to the creaking of the floorboards as she slowly shuffled herself down the stairs, followed by the sound of water filling a kettle and the clatter of mugs. If his gran was up, then he may as well go downstairs too.

At the kitchen table he saw his dad talking to a round bellied man with long bushy sideburns that continued down both cheeks.

'Good morning Joe,' said the other man with a look of sympathy in his eyes. Joe had noticed that a lot with people since his mother had died, almost like they were expecting him to burst into tears at any time, but it had been six years and he preferred to cry on his own, although that was getting less and less as time went on.

'Morning Mr Blundy,' said Joe politely. Gregg Blundy was the desk clerk at the local police station where Joe's dad also worked. Instinctively, Joe went to the kitchen cupboard, took a bowl out and began filling it from a cereal box whilst trying to listen to the men's conversation without it looking too obvious.

Joe's gran placed a mug of tea on top of the note pad on the table for each of the men and affectionately placed a hand on her son's shoulder.

'So what time did he leave?' asked Sergeant Allen to the other man. He moved his cup of tea off the pad of paper and put it on top of a newspaper instead, freeing the paper to write on. He picked up a pen ready to make notes.

'His mother said that he left around about eight o'clock last night. He told her that he had arranged to stay at a friend's house. She watched him go out of the door and said she saw his reflection go past the front window as if he was heading into town.'

'And she didn't check with the friend first?'

'As it was the start of the holidays, she wasn't worried about him staying over someone else's house. She said that she was just glad that Peter had made friends. It wasn't until this morning that she rang the friend's house to see what time he was coming home and apparently he hadn't been there at all.'

'What about other friends? Has she rung around them?'

'Sounds like he didn't really have many friends. Never had anyone over for tea. Used to prefer sitting on his own amongst the long grass of the field behind his house for hours drawing small creatures in his sketchbook. Sounds like a bit of a loner really.'

Sergeant Philip Allen looked out of the kitchen window. It was rare for him to be able to experience the beauty of the orange and pink clouds of a morning sunrise. Although it was early, there was something very beautiful and peaceful about the world at this time of the day, even the two birds tweeting excitedly to each other outside the window seemed to agree. But Sergeant Allen knew that it would not last for long and from what he was hearing it seemed that it was not likely to be a good day. It was unusual for anything to happen in Parsley Bottom except for the odd car accident or minor disturbance, but a missing child was definitely unusual.

'Is there anything missing from his room?' he asked his clerk.

'She's had a look and the only things that are missing are some bedding and his teddy bear. She said he had a small bag with him when he left.'

'So he definitely intended going somewhere for the night,' replied Sergeant Allen.

Joe noticed that his gran had already started to make some sandwiches for his dad, knowing that he would be going into work shortly.

'There is nothing else missing that she can tell; no money or photographs. He had some birthday money stuffed inside an old pottery money box which doesn't appear to have been touched. Also his sketchpad is still in his room,' added PC Blundy.

Sergeant Allen lifted the cup of tea to his lips and took a small sip as he listened once again, wincing as the hot water stung his lip. Despite the burn it felt good feeling the warm liquid dribbling down inside his throat, heating up his stomach.

He chewed the end of the pen as he thought about the information he had already been given and what answers were still needed. Joe brought his bowl over and sat down at the table next to his dad. He purposely munched his cereal slowly so that he could still hear the conversation despite the crunching echoing in his ears.

'And she's checked the loft and shed to make sure he's not hidden in there?'

'She's checked every place she can think of.'

'Are there any other family members he could have stayed with?' They were obvious questions but from what he had read in other missing person reports, children didn't usually go very far from what they were familiar with.

'His dad's away working in the North Sea, he's a welder on the rigs so only comes home every few months. The only other family member is an elderly grandmother and she lives in a nursing home.'

'Had he been acting normally recently? Did he mention anyone new that he'd met?'

'No, but she did mention something a bit strange. She says that she has always felt like they were being watched. I don't know how much of this is in her imagination but apparently, when they had lived in Liverpool, there had often been an elderly man hanging around wherever they went. But when they moved to Parsley Bottom three years ago to care for her mother, she says she still sees the man everywhere only now he has a pointed white beard. But she's sure it's the same person.'

'Might be worth checking it out. Send PC Lloyd round to talk to Mrs Crisp and get a detailed statement as well as a recent photograph of her son. We need some background information; was he having any problems at school that she knew of? Was he happy? Check social services records as well as police records from Liverpool, make sure it's been a happy household and there have been no other reported problems.'

'Will do.'

He took another sip of tea, giving himself time to think of anything else.

'Are there any security cameras near their address? Send someone to ask the local businesses if we can look at their recordings from last night, maybe we can find out which way he headed.'

'Shall I start to organise a search yet?'

'No, let's wait until we find out more before we start an official search. Chances are he's run away, got scared over night and will turn up soon. Let me go and get dressed then we'll go down to the station.'

Sergeant Allen pushed his chair backwards, scraping the legs against the bare floorboards and let out a loud sigh as he climbed the stairs back to the room he shared with his son.

'What have you got planned for the school break Joe?' asked PC Blundy, trying to make conversation while he waited.

'Nothing yet,' replied Joe. 'Was that Peter Crisp's mum you were talking about?'

'Yes, do you know him?'

'Peter's in my class at school,' answered Joe in between spoons of cereal. 'What's happened to him?'

'He's gone missing. What's he like at school?'

'Well, he doesn't really have that many friends, if that's what you mean, but he seems ok, never got into any trouble,' replied Joe.

'I think we've got a picture of him somewhere,' said Mrs Allen. She went through a doorway into the lounge where she kept Joe's school photographs propped up on the mantelpiece and took a cardboard backed photograph from the top of the mantelpiece and brought it back into the kitchen. She placed it on the table in front of Joe and PC Blundy.

'That's him there isn't it Joe?' she asked, pointing a bony finger at a boy standing at the back of the photograph alongside the other tall members of his class. He had an unwashed appearance to his face and thick, untidy brown hair that flopped over his glasses. Whilst all the other faces looked down the camera lens with a smile and youthful confidence, Peter appeared to stand slightly separate from the rest of the class, a distance in his eyes like he knew a secret that no one else could guess. Joe nodded as he scraped the spoon around the bottom of his cereal bowl scooping up what remained of the milk from his breakfast.

'May I borrow this?' asked PC Blundy.

'As long as we get it back,' replied the elderly woman with a knowing smile on her lips.

As soon as he was allowed to leave the house Joe grabbed his jacket, got on his bike and cycled over to his best friends' house. He took the bike around the outside of the house and knocked on the back door.

Max's mum, who could always be found in the utility room sorting out the clean and dirty clothes for Max and his four older sisters, opened the door almost immediately and greeted Joe with a warm and friendly smile.

'Morning Joe, you're out and about early,' she said.

'Morning Mrs Scott,' replied Joe as he kicked his shoes off at the door and rushed past her. He always felt welcome at Max's house and one more person in a house of seven didn't really make much difference to Mrs Scott, who was always pleased to see him.

He leapt up the staircase two at a time towards his friend's bedroom, knocked once and walked straight in. A blond haired boy was sat at a desk with a thick text book open in front of him, an even heavier book resting on the pages to keep it open at the right page.

'Hi Joe,' greeted Max as he looked up from the text book, 'I thought I'd make a start on the maths homework.'

'Max, it's the first day of the holiday, why have you started your homework already?'

'I don't think I've got these percentages right,' he said ignoring Joe's question.

Max's room was always tidy and organised. His desk had everything neatly arranged in square piles. Pens were colour coded and arranged by height and were lined up perfectly straight at the side of the desk. His books were lined up in the same way on his shelf and his duvet had been neatly tucked in around his mattress.

Joe carefully closed the bedroom door behind him then sank into the bean bag next to the desk.

'Are you alright?' asked Max looking strangely at his friend, noticing the look of excitement on Joe's face.

'Peter Crisp has gone missing! His mum contacted my dad and he's gone down to the police station to start to look for him,' said Joe in an excited but quiet voice so that no one else could hear him.

Max shook his head.

'No, he's down at the church graveyard,' said Max unimpressed. 'I heard him talking to Jimmy Cox at school yesterday. Everyone knows how Peter wants to fit in so Jimmy dared him to stay there the night.'

'Oh,' Joe's excitement ended pretty quickly. 'Well he's going to be in big trouble when his mum finds him.'

'Maybe we should tell your dad.'

'Why don't we go over to the graveyard and see if he's still there? We could at least warn him that his mum's looking for him so he can think up some excuse.'

'I suppose so,' said Max unconvinced.

Joe stood up and closed Max's text book for him, leaving his pencil in the central fold as a marker for later then started heading out of the house through the utility room. Max had no option but to follow, shouting goodbye to his mum, who had now started on the ironing.

4. THE SECRET MEETING

There were three other people in the room apart from himself; Sir Adam, the tall scar faced man from the lift and another man, who's suit was so badly crumpled it looked like he had gone to sleep in it, although the dark bags under his eyes indicated that he rarely got enough sleep.

'Good morning Mr Knight, thank you for agreeing to meet with us,' said the crumpled man. Inwardly Steven laughed at the man's comment, he hadn't had much choice about going there, but he decided not to say anything. 'My name is Seward,' he continued. The name rang a bell inside Steven's head, but he couldn't quite put his finger on where he had heard it before. 'What we are about to tell you is top secret and should be protected at all costs.' He paused, waiting to see if Steven understood the importance of what he had said whilst he turned a laptop round so everyone could see the presentation that he had started.

'Meteorites,' Seward said as a way of an introduction. 'Unless they are very large, many meteorites land on the Earth's surface unnoticed.' Different slides of meteorites appeared on the screen of the laptop illustrating his story. 'Stone meteorites are the most common type and can often be difficult to recognise from the rocky surface they land on. Stone meteorites are divided into Chondrites and Achondrites. It's the Achondrites that interest us today Mr Knight. You may not know that they are often pieces from mature planets or moons and travel the solar system for millions of years before landing on Earth.' The slide show continued to show pictures of meteorites travelling through space.

'Have you heard of the Antarctic Mars Meteorite, or ALH84001,' interrupted Sir Adam. Steven nodded. He remembered reading about a meteorite that had been found in Antarctica in 1984. It was memorable because of the fossils inside it.

'ALH8401 was thought to be about 4 billion years old. There were reports that it contained fossilised Martian microbes, microscopic life forms that sparked excitement about the existence of extra terrestrial life.'

'You may recall the spectacular meteor shower we had over the skies of the UK several months ago. The meteors were from Tuttle's Comet. Most meteorites are as small as grains of sand and disintegrate in the Earths atmosphere. But this shower was different. The British Government has recently acquired a small rock no bigger than a large pebble that landed in a town called Parsley Bottom in Yorkshire. On its impact to Earth the outer layer fractured open and split into two parts.' Seward took a charcoal black hemi-sphere rock out of his pocket and placed it on the table in front of them all. 'This is one half of that rock.'

Steven picked it up. He could feel the smoothness of its surface with his finger tips, punctured by small holes like popped bubbles. On the flat edge was an uneven crystal surface with a honeycomb appearance at the centre, its colours radiated out in an ever darkening way to the charred surface.

'Meteorites land on our planet every month,' Sir Adam took over once again, 'but this one has caused great interest. The core of the meteorite contained traces of a substance that we are unable to identify.'

'You mean it contained something we've never seen on this planet before?' asked Steven.

'Exactly.'

'But, I thought that Meteorites became so hot as they entered the atmosphere that nothing could survive?' interrupted Steven.

'You're correct,' Seward began again, 'a meteor is subjected to intense heat as it enters the Earth's atmosphere and many harmlessly burn up. These high temperatures are enough to destroy any substance on the surface of the meteor. In fact the rock actually begins to melt at its surface.' He lifted up the half of meteorite that was on the table, 'during its long journey through cold space the inside of the meteorite would have become frozen. Although the crust would have become hot and melted in our atmosphere, the temperature of the core remains relatively low.'

'So what was inside the meteorite?' Steven bravely asked.

'Whatever it is, it hasn't been seen on Earth, until now,' the scar faced man spoke with a deep American accent.

'This is Coldred,' Sir Adam indicated to the scar faced man. 'His speciality is Biochemical Engineering.'

'What did the analysis report say?' Steven asked.

'The meteorite crust is mainly made of rock with traces of iron and various minerals. More importantly, there was something inside the core. My research and development team have been working on the core of the other half. Inside, was what appeared to be a basic form of bacteria, but one that was different to any we've seen before. We found the bacteria deep inside the core away from the split. The original samples were lost as the bacteria seemed to dry and shrink when exposed to daylight, so we now only handle it in a strict environment; total darkness, 80% humidity with Night Vision goggles for our technicians. In a dark environment the bacteria changes at an alarming rate. Upon first being discovered it was given the code McRae01, named after the man who found it, but the bacteria has been changing, almost evolving, so much so that we have had to rename it several times, the differences are so great. The version we had growing in the laboratory when I left it this morning was coded McRae32-4.' There was silence in the room, as the relevance of Coldred's last statement sank into Steven's brain; the bacteria was changing rapidly.

'Why is it changing?'

'It's adapting and feeding. I've never seen a bacteria change at such a rate. It almost appears to be evolving before our eyes every time the cells of the bacteria split and divide,' replied Coldred.

'A recent sample of the local river water also showed traces of a similar bacteria,' interrupted Seward.

'But how could it have got there? Have any other meteorites been discovered in the area?' Steven noticed how none of the men had any notes, obviously they wanted their meeting kept on a strictly unofficial basis.

'None yet. But it seems logical that there could be more,' answered Seward. 'There have also been reports of small animals, rats and water voles, appearing dead along the banks of Parsley Bottom River. We can assume that they had been drinking the water from the river, which unknown to themselves slowly poisoned them, their bodies unable to cope with this new bacteria.'

Coldred added another shocking piece of information. 'In the last week we have also received another more worrying report. A local farmer sent some of his cows to the abattoir to be slaughtered for the meat market, but the butcher at the abattoir noticed that the meat inside one of the animal's was an unusual colour, almost like it was decaying from the inside. I took some blood samples and the test results showed the same bacteria, but it had changed even more rapidly than the one in our laboratory. These samples also showed some similarities to another bacteria that we already have on Earth called Streptococcus Pyogenes. You may have seen it in the newspapers before; the tabloids call it the "flesh-eating bacteria.".'

5. THE STATUE OF SAINT VITUS

Parsley Bottom Church was not far from Max's house so it didn't take them long to reach the hanging gate that led into the graveyard. They lay their bikes on the sloped grass verge off the road and looked over the small stone wall.

'Doesn't look like anyone's here,' said Max.

'No,' replied Joe. 'It's very quiet isn't it? Why is it that graveyards always seem to be so quiet? I can't even hear any birds.'

A cold stale smell mixed with the earthy scent of damp decaying leaves drifted across the graveyard towards Joe and Max, heavy like a sheet of fog floating across the sea. Joe leant on his hands as he tried to peer further over the wall. The evening frost had melted in the morning sun leaving the soft moss cold and wet against his skin. He quickly removed his hands from the wall and wiped them on his jeans.

'Peter!!!' shouted Joe, his voice echoed off the side of the church, 'It's Joe Allen. Where are you?'

A rustling sound from the grass verge on the opposite side of the lane made Joe and Max turn around suddenly thinking that Peter was behind them, but they couldn't see anyone.

'Come on,' said Joe as he started to push the gate open. The bottom edge of the gate bit into the overgrown ground leaving a deep scar in the mossy earth. Joe entered first, followed more slowly and nervously by Max.

'Peter!' Joe shouted again. 'Are you sure he was coming here?' he asked Max as he constantly looked around him, expecting Peter to jump out.

'Definitely. Look over there.' Max pointed to the corner of a blanket poking out from behind a gravestone. They walked round only to find an untidy bundle of fabric made up of what looked like a blanket and sleeping bag. 'If Peter's not been here then someone else certainly was.'

'If that is Peter's sleeping bag, what's it covered in? Look at that!' Joe prodded a silvery covering of slime with the end of a stick. It seemed to be all over the lower part of the sleeping bag as well as around the bottom of some of the gravestones. 'It looks like the frothy spit from a dog's mouth.'

'Maybe he brought his dog with him?'

'I don't think he has one,' replied Joe.

They followed the slimy trail towards the side of the church nearest to the river. The ground around here appeared to have been dug recently and there were scratch marks in the mud as if a dog had been digging in the wet soil. Some of the ground had been moved away from the lower stones in the church wall and around the edges of this an opening had been created. The slime appeared to be thicker in the entrance to the opening.

Joe leant down and tried to peer into the hole but the smell that came from inside was harsh and felt like it was burning the back of his nose. He quickly pulled his head away and held the collar of his shirt over his mouth and nose to prevent himself from breathing in any more.

'Could you see anything?' asked Max from a safe distance behind.

'No,' said Joe, 'but it smells really bad in there and it's too small for anyone to climb into. Maybe a fox has got trapped and died,' he added unconvinced. They both turned away and started to walk back towards the bundle of clothes they had found behind the gravestone, not realising that they were being watched.

'Look over there,' said Max to Joe, 'what's that?' He pointed towards a brown shape with a red stripe near to the thick wooden door of the church. They both moved towards it, bypassing the jumble of blankets near the gravestone. Max was beginning to feel uncomfortable and guilty about being there. He looked all around the graveyard hoping that no one had noticed them; the last thing he wanted was to get into trouble.

'Shouldn't we go back and tell your dad?' Max said hopefully.

As they approached the brown shape, it began to look more recognisable as a teddy bear. Joe picked it up.

'Dudley,' he read the name on the label that stuck out from behind the red scarf on its neck. 'Mrs Crisp said that there was bedding and his teddy bear missing from his room at home.'

'Well, Peter was definitely here then. Can we go now Joe, graveyards give me the creeps,' Joe asked, trying not to think about all of the dead bodies under the ground.

'Wait, the church doors are open, he may have changed his mind and gone to sleep inside instead of staying out here all night.' The grain on the old wooden doors was worn deep and cut into the wood like claw marks on a tree. It was studded with black iron rivets, some of which had gone rusty and leaked a dark stain in the wood beneath them. There was a small plastic sign screwed onto the door above the handle telling them that the church was closed and that visitors should go to Manor Cottage to obtain the key. But today the door appeared to be already open.

Joe pushed against the heavy door which, despite its weight, swung smoothly inwards. There was a metallic grinding from the hinge and the metal knocker made a loud clang as it swung back and hit against the door, echoing inside the empty church.

Joe took a step inside the stone porch of the church where the air seemed cold and slightly damp. 'Come on. Let's check in here, if there's no sign of him we'll go,' he said to Max who was still standing outside.

'Are you sure we're allowed in there, the sign says it's closed? It's not a Sunday or anything, so maybe we shouldn't go in. What if someone finds us, they may think we're vandalising it or something. My dad would kill me!'

'But the door's unlocked. Don't worry so much, we're only trying to find Peter,' Joe reassured Max as he pushed the door shut behind them before opening the inner door to the church.

Max took small steps behind Joe who now stood behind rows and rows of wooden benches. On the table in front of Max were piles of hymn books stacked neatly, as well as an empty metal collection plate and some printed pieces of paper with information about the Church. The air inside the tall space smelt stale and dusty.

'Peter,' shouted Joe once again, but slightly quieter than he had outside.

'Careful where you're standing,' Max warned Joe as he looked down at the floor. Beneath Joe's trainers was a similar clear slime on the floor to that which they had seen around the hole and sleeping bag outside.

'It goes down here,' said Joe as he pointed to a trail of slime that led down between the benches, 'come on.'

Max lifted up the bottom of his shoes to make sure he hadn't walked in anything then followed, being much more cautious about where he stood than Joe and gingerly stepped around the trail of slime towards the far end of the church.

The giant empty cavern of the inside of the church made each sound echo all around them. Occasionally they would hear the odd creak or crack from the wooden beams supporting the roof above which would make them look up nervously. Stone carved faces looked back down at the two boys disapprovingly and the stained glass window at the far end of the church cast twisted coloured shapes onto the stone walls.

The slime looked like it had been dragged along the smooth stone floor towards a separate part of the building to the right of the main length of the church which is where Joe now stood in front of a large stone statue. A lot more slime had collected around the grey stone base and above was a statue of a young boy towering over Joe. Around the boy's head soft faced angels flew weightlessly, frozen in stone. Looking down from the angels Joe noticed that the boy seemed to have the lower part of his body inside a round pot with solid stone flames licking up from around the bottom.

'Saint Vitus,' said Max reading from the brass plaque at the base of the statue. 'Who's he? And why is he in a cooking pot?'

Joe looked down at the slime around the base of the statue, ignoring Max's questions.

'Anyway, it looks like Peter's not here either,' said Max.

'Why would there be a lot more of that slime around this statue and not the others?' thought Joe aloud as he crouched down to take a closer look.

'I don't know. Maybe some dogs came into the church and dribbled on the floor?' Max was getting nervous again and wanted to go as soon as possible, so he just said the first thing that entered his head, 'maybe they all sleep in here or were waiting for something.'

'It all seems a bit strange to me. It smells like the slime from around that hole outside. And anyway, how would a dog open the front door?'

'Well, someone must have let the dogs in and maybe they followed the person to here? What are you doing now?'

Joe had started to climb onto the stone base, but his trainers were slippery from standing on the slime so he kicked them off. The loud slapping sound they made as they hit the floor rebounded off the church walls making Max jump and nervously look around. Joe managed to get his left foot onto the thick lip of the cooking pot and by pushing his back up against the church wall he levered his right leg up and around the statue. He was now standing behind the statue with his feet on the edge of the pot and his arms around the neck and shoulders of the stone boy. First he looked down towards Max, who was now telling him that standing on statues was a really bad idea and God would probably punish them both for it, but then he looked around the statue itself. There was a mark on the wall just above his head. It looked like a badly drawn circle with several lines sticking out from the edge. He traced his finger in the shallow scratch then noticed that there were also two scratched letters inside the circle. Although there was a slight shadow cast underneath the wall, Joe was sure that the letters were P and C.

Where Joe's own feet were balanced on the statue he could see some muddy marks and down at the base of the cooking pot behind the statue, was what looked like a metallic chocolate bar wrapper catching a little of the light that came through one of the small leaded windows above.

'Peter's definitely been here, his initials are scratched on the wall and there's a chocolate wrapper down here.'

'The wrapper could have been there for ages,' replied Max.

'But there are muddy foot marks here too, and the mud's still soft.' Joe almost slipped off the statue as he heard the clang of the metal door knocker bang against the outer door.

Someone was entering the church.

'Come on,' said Max in a quiet shout as Joe leapt off the statue to land next to his friend. He quickly grabbed his trainers from the floor then they both crept to peep past the side wall and look down the length of the church towards the entrance. Joe could almost feel the pulse in his neck pumping so hard that it made his head shake. They couldn't see anyone but they could hear that someone was now inside the church by the loud wheezing breaths they took and the knocking sound of a wooden stick against the stone floor.

'What are we going to do? I told you we weren't allowed in here.'

Joe continued to look down the church. A figure of an old man slowly walked into view, he was dressed in a neat brown suit and had a white goatee beard that rested in a point on his chest.

'Who's he?' whispered Max into Joe's ear.

'I don't know, but Mrs Crisp said that she had seen a white bearded man watching them, do you think that could be him?'

A faint whisper echoed near to where Joe and Max were.

'Pssst.'

Joe looked at Max with a confused look on his face and silently mouthed the words, 'what was that?' Max shrugged his shoulders, he had heard it too.

'Hey!' The whisper was slightly louder and Joe realised where it was coming from. On the opposite side to their hiding place was a small wooden door where a red haired girl was signalling for them to come over to her.

'Who's she?' asked Max.

'Whoever she is, I think I'd rather go with her. That must be another way out.'

To get to the door would mean crossing the centre of the length of the church, where no benches would hide them. Joe had an idea. He crouched down until he could see all the way to the other end of the church by looking underneath all of the benches. If he could see the feet of the person who had just come in he would know where he was and which direction he was facing so that they could cross to the red headed girl.

They waited.

He could see the feet at the table with the hymn books on but then they shuffled and disappeared behind a thick stone pillar. A few seconds later they reappeared at the hymn book bench again but a sheet of paper fluttered down to land on the floor next to the feet. Joe froze, if the person bent down low enough, they would be able to look back at Joe and their hiding place would be discovered. He held his breath not daring to move. With an obvious effort, the person slowly knelt down and rested their body weight on a long bony hand whilst the other scratched at the corner of the piece of paper to make it easier to lift.

This was their chance. Quietly Joe and Max crawled quickly along the length of the bench across the open central area and back behind the benches on the other side of the church. On their knees they then crawled towards the red haired girl who opened the door a little wider to let them through.

Back at the hymn book table the man suddenly stopped wheezing and lifted his head above the bench to look intently towards the small door that Joe and Max had just passed through. The face was old and wrinkled with small blue eyes staring out from underneath the thick white eyebrows and, despite the appearance of the aged body, there was an inner strength that seemed to radiate from it. He took a long sniff of the air before standing upright and following the trail of slime down the centre of the church towards the statue.

Joe and Max ran down a narrow dark passageway, towards a light that came from another small door that led outside. No one dared say anything until they were out in the fresh air, then Max let out a long gasp of nervous breath.

'Thanks,' said Joe, who was still holding his trainers, to the red headed girl.

'Your welcome,' she said smiling, 'I'm Scarlet. I saw you looking around the graveyard from up in that tree. That's my dad's land over there,' she pointed to the wooded area across the river. 'You looked like you had lost something, so I thought I'd come over to see if I can help. What's wrong with your trainers?'

Joe looked down at them. The rubber soles under the trainers seemed to be melting. Carefully he scraped them against the side of a gravestone leaving a trail of soft black rubber on the edge.

'It looks like they've melted,' Scarlet said.

Joe lifted them up to sniff them then pulled his face away from the acidic smell.

'It must be the slime you stood in,' Max said to Joe, who had now begun wiping them on some wet grass. All that was left of the sole was a thin layer of rubber where, in patches, it was bare to the white lining on the inside.

'This is getting stranger all the time,' said Joe, 'and where is Peter?'

6. NEWTON RISE ABATTOIR

Three miles away from Parsley Bottom on the road to Harrogate was the slightly larger town of Newton Rise, a farm town which regularly held a cattle market in the main square every Wednesday. The farmers markets had become a regular tourist attraction in the summer where anything could be bought from local honey and fresh breads to prize winning cattle and waxed jackets. Pedestrians walked along the pavements past the sandstone clad shops while motorists respectfully drove slowly along the narrow roads simply to admire the buildings and be part of the uniqueness of a country town.

Away from the town the old abattoir was a boring grey concrete building protected by a high boundary wall with black iron gates barring the entrance. At the front of the building were two large shutters big enough to admit lorries in, whilst on the right side a covered walkway led from a field at the back into the main building. By contrast the interior of the building shone white and gleamed with the steel machinery.

In the staff canteen a man sat hunched over his cup of steaming tea at the first table nearest the doors. There weren't many people in the canteen at this time of the afternoon and he was happy to have some time away from his work colleagues and rest his weary body on the plastic chair. He had already tried to eat a packet of biscuits but today he couldn't keep anything inside his stomach, it seemed to be permanently tight like someone had reached inside him and wouldn't stop squeezing.

He pulled out a tissue from his trouser pocket and wiped his nose. Before returning it to his pocket he checked the tissue for more signs of blood.

Gilbert Rackham had been working at the abattoir since he was just 17 years old after being encouraged to follow in his father's footsteps. He didn't particularly enjoy the work he did but at least it paid his bills and kept food on the family table. He would probably keep working there until the day he retired. But, the work had changed over the last few years and instead of being an important part of the market town, the abattoir was becoming a symbol for animal cruelty and on occasions Gilbert's children had been bullied by their school friends who didn't agree with their father's job.

As he sat at the table playing with the salt and pepper shakers, he thought back to the strange events of the last few weeks after he had noticed something unusual about a cow that had come from Parsley Bottom. So much had happened since then. After four hours the cow had been removed from the building and he had been interviewed twice by official looking men, as well as having all of his clothes removed and swabs taken from his skin and fingernails. He had asked why so much precaution was necessary, but no one would give him an answer, he was just forced to do as he was told.

Gilbert tried to think about the meat he had seen and what it was that made it so different to a normal cow, except for the strange dark colouring of the flesh inside. There had been no reports from any of his colleagues about the cow acting unusual, and all of the other cows from the same herd had seemed normal. So why was this cow so different?

His mind wandered back to the canteen that he was sat in. He didn't know what was happening to him recently. He seemed to have no energy despite wanting to eat more than usual and he had a constant ache in his legs and arms. Every morning it was getting worse, but he didn't want to mention it to his wife, it was probably just his age or maybe he was coming down with the flu. He had even noticed that the skin on his hands was getting thinner and showed the bones beneath more clearly.

As he sat there he noticed that his breathing was becoming quite hard and all he could manage were short shallow breaths. He screwed his eyes up tight trying to clear the fog from his vision but it never changed. His hearing was also becoming muffled and distant. He tried to focus on the large white faced clock on the wall at the end of the canteen but it seemed to swim in mid air before him. He could just about make out the black hands telling him that he only had 5 minutes of his break to go before he would have to get back on the work floor. Gilbert decided to freshen up as much as possible so that he could see his day through to the end and not loose any of his pay.

He struggled to get to his feet. By holding on to the wall he slowly made his way through the double doors into the locker room looking like a crooked old man. He found his locker amongst the sea of other identical metallic grey boxes and fumbled with the key as he tried to get it into the small lock. He felt his forehead with the back of his hand; it was cold and wet. He took a box of pain killers out of his bag and pushed two tablets out of their silver pockets and into his hand.

An overwhelming feeling like a wave of shivering heat washed across the surface of his body and his legs collapsed from beneath him. By the time his body hit the floor Gilbert was already dead. His still open eyes turned a milky colour, his heart stopped, his lungs could no longer suck air into his body and his muscles had wasted away, eaten by an unknown bacteria that fed on his flesh to grow and consume his body.

Unknown to Gilbert, the bacteria had transferred from the cow's meat under his fingernails and into his mouth. The rest of the staff at the Abattoir had also picked up the bacteria off the work surfaces, handrails and doorknobs that Gilbert had touched, as well as through the air he had sneezed and coughed into and they would slowly go the same way as Gilbert, his wife and their two daughters.

Unless something could be done about it, this unknown bacteria would continue to spread in the same way from staff to their families and very quickly it would consume humans to develop into a species all of its own.

7. LONDON TO YORK

Steven left the MI6 building and walked across Vauxhall Bridge Road towards the nearest underground station. A sharp breeze blew off the Thames, stinging his cheeks, but he welcomed the fresh air after spending an hour inside the windowless box of a room with the other men.

During that one meeting his belief in alien life forms had been renewed. Even though the bacteria from inside the meteorite was only the most basic of life forms, it was still alien to this planet.

He entered Pimlico underground station and jumped on the first train towards Kings Cross. Whilst the tube train rattled along the track in bouts of acceleration and deceleration, Steven pulled out the train ticket to Parsley Bottom he had been issued with before leaving the meeting. After a few minutes he arrived at Kings Cross Station and began picking his way through the crowd of people whilst looking at the departures board for his train, making a mental note of the platform number. Once inside the train he found a seat with a table and looked out of the window at his fellow passengers dragging luggage trolleys or children quickly up the platform, to avoid missing the train's departure.

Other passengers entered the carriage, some sat down whilst others moved through into the next carriage. Steven was grateful that no one came and sat at the table, he preferred a bit of privacy. As the whistle blew and the train started to pull its way out of the station, Steven looked around the carriage, every one else was settled in their seats ready for the 2 hour journey to York. He had been instructed that he would be met at York station ready for the drive towards Harrogate and Parsley Bottom. He sat back in his seat and relaxed, but his mind kept wandering back to the meeting inside the MI6 building.

The fact that the bacteria was changing so rapidly was incredible, but what was even scarier was its ability to eat flesh.

'What would bacteria usually eat?' Steven had asked Seward when he was in the enclosed room.

'Bacteria are decomposers; they eat things like Algae, and Fungi as well as dead skin cells and hair. Instead of using a mouth they produce enzymes that break down the food into smaller parts, just like the acid inside your stomach would. Some bacteria will only eat one type of food, whilst others are able to eat several different types.'

The deep voice of Coldred interrupted his colleague. 'But they can adapt to their environment. Bacteria that can't break down one type of food will live next to other bacteria that can.'

'So why was this alien bacteria found inside the body of a cow? Shouldn't it have been living on decomposing animals or leaves or something?'

'Most bacteria would, but don't forget this is new to this planet, it acts in different ways to Earth bacteria,' replied Seward. 'There are several possibilities how it could have got into the cow. It could have drunk from the river, consuming the bacteria then it started to eat the flesh after the cow had died. The second possibility is the cleanliness at the abattoir could be below standard and the bacteria may have been introduced on the blade of the knife, which then started to multiply and divide on the flesh.'

'But how could the bacteria be on the blade in the first place? You're avoiding the most likely explanation,' said Coldred who didn't appear to be convinced and seemed to be frustrated by Seward's explanations. He didn't wait for an answer before continuing with his own opinion. 'The other possibility is that it was already eating the cow from the inside *before* it died.' They all turned towards Coldred. Except for his deep voice echoing in their heads, the room was silent.

Seward and Sir Adam looked uncomfortably at each other; Steven thought that maybe Coldred had said too much.

'Are you saying that the bacteria was eating him alive?' Steven asked in amazement.

'We don't know that for sure,' Seward quickly spoke, preventing Coldred answering. 'This bacteria just acts differently to ones we have on this planet,' he continued, providing this as an explanation for Steven.

There was tension in the room. Steven wanted to move the subject on and pretend that he hadn't noticed the importance of what Coldred had said. Sometimes he found that it was better to act stupid to avoid any complications that understanding could cause. However, inside his mind he was thinking that if the bacteria had got in the cow and was eating it, it would probably mean that the bacteria had killed the cow by attacking it from the inside. It didn't just eat dead cells and fungus, but could attack an animal and silently pick the living flesh from the bones from the inside without the animal knowing. This was a complicated and much more deadly bacteria to any that had been found on Earth.

'What happened to the cow?' Steven asked casually, trying to act normal.

Coldred looked at Seward, almost waiting to receive the go ahead to answer the question, he was obviously aware of his disapproval over his last outburst. Seward nodded to Coldred who then answered. 'I have it at my laboratory. Some of my staff are observing the process of the bacteria eating the flesh as we speak.' Coldred then turned to Seward, 'a full report should be ready shortly,' he said as if he was trying to gain back some approval from Seward.

After talking briefly about the importance of secrecy, he had been instructed by Sir Adam to go to Parsley Bottom and look for evidence of any other meteorites that may have fallen, as well as talk to Mr McRae, the man that had found the original meteorite. Although they had provided some enlightening information, Steven felt that there was a lot more that he wasn't being told. He remembered what Sir Adam had said on the walk to the meeting, *'do not trust everything and everyone you are about to meet. What you are about to see is only half the story. There are things they won't tell you.'* Steven definitely hadn't liked Coldred, there was something strange about him, his eyes seemed to stare icily into your head, reading what your brain was thinking.

'But why me?' Steven had asked.

'We don't want panic,' answered Sir Adam, 'just a polite and innocent investigation. Out of all the members of the UFA team you are the one I choose. You are the one I can trust. We don't want the army ploughing in causing chaos and panic. For now we need to determine how far the bacteria has spread. Find as many meteorite samples as you can and try to establish an area that may have become effected by the bacteria.'

'Because the bacteria doesn't seem to react well to sunlight, we don't think it will be able to survive for long in the open. Look for dead or sick animals, talk to the farmers and take water samples. Overall, this is an unofficial investigation and that's the way I want it to remain,' Seward had instructed him.

The train continued on its journey to York, the rocking motion of the carriage together with the constant hum of the metal wheels against the track, made Steven want to close his eyes. Despite trying to resist it, the heavy eyelids slid over his eyes and his body leant back against the seat and he relaxed into sleep. Steven wasn't the only person in the carriage who had dropped off; a university student used her overly large back pack as a pillow against the cold window pane, whilst two children played on handheld computers, their parents completing a crossword together. At the back of the carriage, a grey haired man in a suit was reading today's newspaper; the open pages were large enough to shield his face from everyone else, but occasionally he would drop the paper slightly so that his eyes could see over the top. He would then scan the rest of the occupants in the carriage, but his eyes always seemed to linger on Steven for longer than anyone else. After all, that was what he was being paid to do.

'The next station is York,' announced the recorded voice from inside the carriage.

Steven looked at his watch; he had been asleep for nearly two hours. As he blinked himself awake he stood slowly, arched his stiff back and reached up into the air. The rest of the carriage was now nearly empty except for several people that had collected by the door and were waiting for it to open at the station.

The train slowed and Steven stepped out onto the concrete platform. There was a cold breeze blowing along the tracks towards him and he thought he could feel the odd spit of rain against his cheeks. Pulling the collar of his jacket up around his neck he found a vending machine and selected a chocolate bar to eat as he hadn't had much since breakfast.

'Mr Knight?' came a soft voice from beside him. There was a slight Spanish lisp in the voice which betrayed its origins.

Steven turned to see a slim and beautiful lady in a chocolate brown suit offering a slender hand for him to shake. Her skin had an olive colour to it, even in the grey northern climate. Her full lips gave a cautious smile as she hoped that she had approached the right man.

'Yes,' he blustered, 'I'm Steven Knight.' He took her warm hand gently in his and shook it. He noticed that she was slightly taller than himself, but that could have something to do with height of the shoes she wore.

'My name's Georgia Brown, I'm an MI6 operative assistant. I'm here to take you to Parsley Bottom. A case of clothes has already been arranged for you and is waiting at your accommodation. If you would follow me?'

Before Steven could reply, Georgia had already started walking towards the car park, expecting him to follow. Her golden brown hair bounced gently against her shoulders as she walked gracefully towards a black car. But Steven wasn't the only person watching Georgia. At the other end of the car park the grey haired man from the train already had the engine of his car running, waiting to discreetly follow Steven.

8. A BIRDS EYE VIEW

Max and Joe decided to get away from the church and its visitor for a while so they followed Scarlet over some large stepping stones across the river to the woodland on the other side. Once they had scrambled up the soft bank they found themselves surrounded by the thick harsh trunks of Conifer, Oak and Ash trees. The light from the sky shone through the soft green leaves above them and made the whole place take on a magical green glow. The smell inside the woodland made Max think of Christmas and the pine tree his grandparents always put up in the entrance hall to their home. If he closed his eyes he could almost feel the heat from the fireplace and the excitement in his stomach.

Joe had tried to put his trainers back on but the sole now seemed to be coming away from the rest of the shoe and he almost immediately tripped over, so he decided it would be easier to take them off altogether. Despite the thick layer of brown leaves that covered the ground making it soft and bouncy Joe winced painfully as he felt every stone or bump against his feet.

As they took a few steps forward, the woodland appeared to close in around the children so that they could hardly see where the river and church were.

'Come and climb my tree,' said Scarlet excitedly as she rushed off ahead.

'Who is she?' Joe asked Max.

'I don't know but at least we're not in that creepy church,' Max replied as he followed Scarlet. 'Don't worry about Peter. I bet he's already gone home. He's certainly not in the graveyard anymore,' he shouted as he ran amongst the trees after Scarlet.

'No, I suppose he's not,' said Joe to himself, although he wasn't as easily convinced as Max. It certainly looked like Peter had been in the graveyard at some point then moved into the church. But what was all that slime? Wherever Peter had been, the slime had been too, almost like it had been following him. And the white bearded man? Was he the same one that Mrs Crisp had mentioned to PC Blundy? Then there was that symbol on the wall, the circle with the lines coming out from it, what could that mean? Max seemed happy to think everything was ok, but Joe had a very uneasy feeling in his stomach.

He started to run in the direction the other two had gone, desperately trying to catch a glimpse of Max's blue jacket between the trees. Up ahead he heard the voice of Scarlet calling Max on, but then there was nothing and the only thing he could hear was the rustling sound of leaves being crushed beneath his socks.

Joe looked around him. Everywhere looked the same; he couldn't even tell which way he had just come, all that he could see were grey-green tree trunks with light green leaves. He strained to try to hear something; a voice or a movement, but there was nothing except for the faint whispering of the wind blowing through the tree tops like the woodland was sucking in deep breaths then breathing out heavily.

Suddenly there was darkness.

Something had been put over his head. Joe couldn't see anything. He grabbed at the cover with his hands, desperately trying to get it off but panicked and fell to the ground. As he continued to struggle he finally managed to pull the cover from his head and throw it to the floor. What lay in front of him was Max's coat and above him he could hear giggling coming from the tree above.

'Max!' Joe shouted as he brushed some leaves from his jeans, 'Don't do that!'

'Sorry,' replied Max still laughing. 'Come up here, you can see all over town. I think I can even see your house in the distance.'

Joe grabbed hold of the lowest branch and lifted himself up onto a thicker limb. From there he could see climbing holds drilled into the tree trunk at random positions around the thick trunk, like the shaped grips he had once seen on a climbing wall. It meant that he could scale up the trunk relatively fast to reach the canopy of the tree. There had been some modifications made there too as Max and Scarlet were perched on top of a solid platform made out of a series of wooden planks. He pulled himself onto the platform and punched Max playfully on the shoulder.

'This is great,' he said as he looked over the top of the tree tops down onto the town below.

'My dad made it for me. He got the foot and hand holds at a car boot sale and put them on the tree for me. I often come here and watch the animals. Mainly its just birds you can see but sometimes there's other stuff too. I have a tame grey squirrel that comes up here sometimes and I'm sure I saw a kingfisher the other day on the river down there.' Scarlet pointed down to a spot on the river just south of the graveyard. She unhooked a waterproof bag from a branch next to the platform and took out a sheet of paper. 'Look. I keep a chart of all the animals I've seen,' she said showing Joe and Max who tried not to look too bored.

'How did you know we were in the church?' asked Joe.

'I saw you with these,' Scarlet took a small pair of binoculars out of the bag and showed them to Joe. 'I also saw that man go in shortly after you. Did you know that he had been watching you from the other side of the road since you first arrived? I thought he may be going in to tell you off. You're not supposed to go into the church without going to Mrs Merchant first at Manor Cottage, she has the key. Anyway, I thought I would come and rescue you.'

'Can I have a look?' asked Joe picking up the binoculars from the wooden platform.

'If you look towards the river in the bank beneath the church there's a large hole that wasn't there a few weeks ago. I think there may be otters nesting there or something. Sometimes when the sun's facing in the right direction I can see the dark outlines of animals moving inside it. If it is otters, they must have some pups as well as it seems rather full inside there.'

'There are dogs in there?' Max asked.

'No silly. Pups are baby otters,' replied Scarlet disappointed that Max didn't know as much about otters as she did.

'Why do you come up here?' asked Max.

'This is my father's land; he's Richard Baxley the farmer.'

'I've never noticed you before at school.'

'I go to a Saint Winifred's, the private school over at Otley.'

'Oh,' said Max, feeling slightly inferior.

Joe focused the binoculars on the hole in the river bank which coincidently seemed to be directly below the smaller hole under the church wall that he had looked at earlier. The river bank hole was dug deep into the ground and it appeared to be inky black inside but occasionally his eyes picked out darker shapes moving around from within, as the daylight reflected off the surface of the water and into the hole.

After picking out the landmarks of the town which looked very different from above, the sun got too low in the sky and began to shine in their eyes making it difficult for them to see anything else. Max, Joe and Scarlet made their way back down the tree towards the river crossing then went their separate ways. Max and Joe carefully jumped over the large flat stepping stones back across the river and into the graveyard to collect their bikes. The graveyard was still quiet and as they mounted their bikes Joe took a last uncomfortable look over his shoulder to where the hole underneath the church wall was.

They both cycled along the quiet lane until they got to a junction in the road where they would go off in different directions.

'See you tomorrow,' said Joe.

'Night,' Max shouted from along the road as he cycled home.

Joe arrived home just as his gran was starting to put the cutlery on the dining table for their evening dinner. There were only two place settings, so Joe knew that they would be eating without his father. Whenever this happened Joe would lie awake in his bed and wait to hear a knife and fork clattering against a pottery plate while his father ate his dinner later in the night. He found that he could never go to sleep until he knew that his father was home.

'Dad not back yet?' he asked as his gran took the plates out of the cupboard.

'No, it's just the two of us again. What did you and Max get up to today?'

'Not much,' Joe replied nervously thinking that he was going to be in trouble for going inside the church. 'We went for a bike ride and met a girl called Scarlet on the other side of the river.'

'That's Richard Baxley's land, Scarlet must be his daughter. What happened to your trainers?' she asked Joe as she took a sausage casserole out of the oven.

'The sole came away so it was easier to walk without them on.'

'Well that's what you get for buying cheap trainers, but I'm afraid that's all we can afford at the moment. You'll have to get your old ones out. I know they're a bit small, but they will have to do until we can get you some others.'

'Do you know if dad found Peter Crisp?'

'I haven't heard I'm afraid.'

Joe wanted to talk to his father. He had been wrestling with the decision of whether to tell his dad about what they had seen at the graveyard or not. But, most of all he wanted to ask him if Peter had been found, but it would have to wait until the morning.

It took Joe a long time to get to sleep that night. He had lain awake in his bed moving into the most comfortable position the springs would allow, thinking about the shape he had seen scratched into the wall around the statue in the church. The more he thought about it the more he began to convince himself that the two letters could just have been a trick of the light, making him see things that weren't really there. Or if they were actually letters then maybe it wasn't a P and C, maybe it was a D and L. But it all seemed to fit together. Max said he had definitely heard Peter being dared to sleep in the graveyard by Jimmy Cox and they had found the sleeping bag and blanket as well as his teddy bear, so he must have been there at some point. If it was Peter, why would he climb the statue, it couldn't have been very comfortable to spend the night perched on top of a cold stone statue. It would have been better if he had taken his blanket and sleeping bag into the church and slept on one of the wooden pews. The only thing Joe could think of that would cause someone to spend the night on top of a statue would be if they needed to escape someone or something.

Eventually his brain couldn't think any more and he had finally given in and gone to sleep, but as he lay in his warm soft bed half asleep he suddenly had an idea what the symbol could mean.

9. THE NIGHT WATCHMAN

Bob King was doing his usual hourly checks at the old Parsley Bottom Paper factory for the night. It was cold and he was looking forward to a warm cup of tea and a chocolate biscuit, before settling down for a short nap. Bob had been a night security guard at the factory for just over four years and in that time there had only once been an intruder, if that's what you could call a homeless person looking for somewhere warm to sleep.

The long outside wall of the factory that joined onto the car park was lit by lamps attached from above, and as Bob walked slowly beneath them he moved in and out of the beams like an actor moving across a stage. The only sound that could be heard was the faint metallic chinking sound of the keys loosely hanging around his waist. Bob whistled a nameless tune to accompany his keys and break the silence.

As he came to a door, he tried the handle to make sure that it was locked, before proceeding towards the back of the building. He lifted his wrist and checked the time on his watch, tapping it to make sure that the hands had not got stuck. Ten past two in the morning. He made a note of the time on the chart that was clamped to his clip-board.

At the end of the wall, he turned round and took one final look towards the car park, just to reassure himself that all was secure before moving to the back wall. There were no doors to check on this side of the building and further ahead was the small hut where Bob kept his kettle, biscuits, deck chair and heater. The river ran alongside the back of the factory, moonlight reflected off the surface of the water as it trickled over the stones like last years faulty Christmas tree lights flickering in the night.

Knowing that he had 50 minutes to himself before the next security check at 3am, Bob started to walk a bit quicker, drawn to his hut and the thought of a warm cup of tea.

Suddenly a loud sploshing sound came from the river. He turned and walked slowly and cautiously to the edge of the riverbank, keeping the light from his torch on the ground in front of him so that he could safely see where the drop of the bank started. At the edge he swung the beam of light along the muddy bank then turned it up stream, as well as down.

Nothing.

There are many things that could have made a sploshing sound in the river, such as a small fish jumping out of the water, or an acorn falling from an overhanging oak tree, and Bob's brain automatically came to these conclusions as the most likely reason.

As he turned away from the river to go towards his hut, something caught on the leg of his trousers almost making him lurch forward. Bob's torch fell out of his hand and rolled onto the concrete path. He turned his head to look down at his trouser leg, but something else pulled it from underneath him. He landed heavily on his chest, the breath forced violently out of his lungs. Gasping quick shallow breaths, he tried to look down towards his feet once again, but all he could make out were dark shapes clawing their way up the river bank and clamping themselves tightly around his legs. He tried kicking at them but more were coming out of the water and advancing up his legs. There was a strange, sticky bubbling sound coming from the shapes, getting louder and louder as more of them arrived.

Bob made an attempt to call for help, but he knew that it was useless, after all, he had just checked the grounds around the factory himself and he knew that there was no one else here.

He knew he was on his own.

This feeling of isolation seemed to give Bob an extra boost of energy and his instinctive need to survive kicked in. He tried to grab at whatever was attacking him as it slid towards his chest, but there was nothing solid to get hold of. It was like trying to grab onto a slug. His hands kept slipping off the soft, sticky cold surface that continued to slip through his fingers. He tried instead to pull himself free, gripping the ground above his head with his fingers, feeling the grit and mud gathering under his nails as he clawed desperately at the ground, but it was becoming useless, he was getting nowhere.

By now there was another strange feeling in his legs, but this wasn't on the outside, this felt like it was coming from within his legs, moving like a cold sharp knife through his veins. He tried again to kick the things off, but now found that his legs wouldn't move at all, his brain had stopped controlling them, they were paralysed. In a desperate panic, Bob tried even harder to claw his way out, his fingernails snapping and chipping away on the stones in the mud.

Then began a new feeling; a feeling of intense pain. It felt like someone had poured acid onto the skin of his legs, they were burning and itching so much, all he wanted to do was scratch them. His hands then started to become numb, followed by his tongue which seemed to become as heavy as a lead weight, stopping his cries for help. After all of the chaos and torture, his body became still and calm, he could still hear and see, but he couldn't move any part of his body, not even to blink. Bob could only look at the ground he was lying on whilst the things continued to swamp his body.

They then began to drag Bob into the water. He knew that as soon as his body went into the river and his lungs filled with water he would drown, but even that seemed a good alternative to the agonising burning feeling that now crawled over the flesh of his entire body. As Bob slid down the river bank and into the water, his body rolled so that he was facing upwards, the last thing he saw was the starry sky and the depths of space beyond. The icy water lapped into his mouth and gurgled down into his lungs, before Bob lost consciousness.

The creatures moved quickly over his body, taking what they needed in a wild frenzy, like a lion picking the flesh from a zebra, until there was little left except his wrist watch which floated heavily to rest on the gravel of the river bed.

10. THE FAERIE RING

Unfortunately for Joe, when he woke the following morning, his dad had already left for work again. As soon as he had eaten his breakfast, he wheeled his bike out of the hall, through the front door then cycled along the road in the direction of the church, but this time continued past it. Here the road became a lot narrower and Joe had to ride his bike more carefully to avoid falling into the pot holes that were scattered across the road. It wound its way around farmland edged with high stone walls on both sides. The grey square stones made the walls look fragile as if they could fall down with one small push, especially those that climbed the hill out of town. At the top of the hill he got off his bike and stood for a minute to catch his breath whilst looking out over the patchwork of fields that continued far into the distance away from Parsley Bottom.

Whilst he was trying to get to sleep last night he thought about the symbol he had seen next to the statue and thought that it could indicate the ancient stone circle that stood on the hill overlooking Parsley Bottom. He had decided to go and have a look, but he didn't really know what he was looking for. Any indication that Peter had been there would give Joe more information to pass to his dad.

Joe stopped by the side of a public footpath sign which pointed away from the road and across a field of purple heather. He pushed open a pedestrian field gate and free wheeled his bike through. The strong spring on the post pulled the gate back as soon as Joe let go and it hit the opposite post with a dull thud.

With the bike at his side he walked along the well worn path up the gentle slope towards the stone circle. There was no one else in sight and all Joe could hear was the odd call of a bird carried on the gentle breeze blowing up the hill.

After a while, the heather gave way to a small clearing. The ground here was yellow caused by the dryness of the shallow covering of grass on top of the underlying sandstone. What made this place different to most were the twelve large upright stones that were standing equally spaced and arranged in a circle around two central stones.

This was what Joe thought could have been the shape scratched in the church wall; The Faerie Ring, Parsley Bottom's smaller version of Stonehenge. But why would Peter draw this? Did he leave the church and come here? If so he didn't appear to be here anymore.

Joe put his bike on the ground and walked up to the first of the stones, all of which were about twice the height of him. The surface of the stones was made up of a mixture of greys and browns and had been worn smooth over the years by the constant wind and rain that blew across the Yorkshire countryside. Tufts of moss poked out from the cracks in the stone where rain water had collected. The stones seemed to stick out of the ground at awkward angles and all of them appeared to have something carved on their outer pointing face.

Joe stepped up to the stone nearest the footpath and looked at the unusual writing that was scratched on the surface.

It didn't mean anything to him so he walked across the centre of the circle towards another stone on the other side. This one looked a lot redder in colour and had a narrower base compared to the width at the top. Again he looked up at the writing.

This was the first time that Joe had actually been up close to the stones, although he had often seen them from a distance or heard about them at school, but now that he was standing amongst them he felt a strange feeling come over him almost like an electrical energy that caused static to crackle in the air.

'Interesting place this,' said the voice of an old man who had also walked up to the circle. Joe hadn't noticed him at first and was quite surprised to hear another human voice in the empty air. But he was even more surprised when he turned to look and saw that it was the white bearded man that had followed them into the church.

The old man was standing at the entrance to the circle near to where Joe had left his bike. He leant on an old twisted walking stick and was dressed in the same brown suit as the previous day. He stayed where he was and didn't approach any closer towards Joe who now moved towards the two central stones, cautiously keeping an eye on the man whilst still looking for any evidence of Peter.

'Do you know the story behind this place?' asked the old man who had now sat wearily on the top of a smooth lower stone, almost like he was settling himself down for a long conversation.

Joe tried to remember what he had heard at school, although it probably wouldn't be as much as Max would know if he had been there.

'Isn't it to do with the moon or something?' replied Joe.

'That's what your teachers will say about most stone circles, but this has a different story and one you might find interesting,' he paused before adding, 'especially if you've lost something.'

Joe looked quickly over to the old man, trying to think what he could mean by his last comment. Did he know anything about Peter? How could he know that Joe had come up here looking for Peter? The old man's striking blue eyes seemed to focus sharply on Joe like a hawk on a rabbit.

'Look at the inscriptions on those two stones you're standing next to. They read Belphoebe and Gawain.'

Joe cautiously looked up at the inscriptions:

'They are written in Anglo Saxon Runic symbols. Sir Gawain was the nephew of King Arthur and one of the famous Knights of the Round Table, whilst Belphoebe was a beautiful Faerie princess from the underworld,' continued the old man. 'We are standing on what remains of Lud's Chapel where the marriage of Gawain and Belphoebe was taking place. Standing in front of them is Bishop Baldwin and surrounding the happy couple are eleven of Gawain's friends and fellow knights; Lionel, Dodinal, Gaheris, Bedivere,

Erec, Bors, Ywain, Lamorak, Balin, Lucan and finally Morholt.' He passed his hand round the circle like he was introducing old friends at a dinner party; there was a certain amount of kindness in his voice as he fondly retold the Knight's names.

'But they're just stones,' said Joe disbelieving what the old man had said. He had no way of knowing if what the old man had said about the inscriptions was correct or not.

'It's true, they are stones but they hadn't always been that way. The marriage between a Faerie and a human was strictly forbidden so the Faerie Queen cursed them and their guests by turning them to stone. But in doing so what she actually did was to create a magical place where the human world and the unseen Faerie world are constantly joined, protected by these eleven brave knights as well as Bishop Baldwin, as gods representative on Earth.'

'But I thought Faeries are small things with wings?'

'No. You've been reading too many comic books. The ancient Faeries are shape changers, they can be anything they want to be and can fly by using magic not by papery wings on their back,' replied the old man with a look of annoyance on his face.

'So why would this be a good place to find something you might have lost?' asked Joe, taking the old man back to his earlier comment.

'You came here looking for Peter Crisp didn't you?' he asked.

'How do you know?' replied Joe with surprise.

'He came here two nights ago to hide from something. I'm not sure what it was but there was something in the graveyard with him, I thought you and your friend might know what it was.'

'We know you had been watching us.'

'Your red haired saviour told you did she?' he said with a smile.

'Yes. So where is Peter now?'

'I don't know,' the old man sadly replied. 'I should have been there to help him but now he's gone. He passed on from here.'

'Where to?' Max asked.

'Legend has it that this circle is actually an entrance to the Underworld. That's where he's gone.'

11. THE LEAGUE OF WHITE KNIGHTS

Joe felt uncomfortable and wanted to get away from the man as soon as possible, but the old man was still sitting on the stone nearest to the footpath and more importantly next to his bike. His exit was blocked. How could the old man know about Peter, unless he was somehow involved with his disappearance? The old man was talking about tales and stories from medieval days when they also believed in Dragons and the bogey monster, but now everyone knew there were no such things as Faeries, especially ones that could turn things into stone.

'If this is an entrance to somewhere, then where's the door?' he asked looking around the circle pretending he'd missed it but secretly looking to see if there was any other way to escape. All around the circle was farmland, he was sure that he could outrun the old man, after all he needed a stick just to walk.

'You can't see the door. It's an energy field that can only be opened in one of three ways. The first way is by being the possessor of the Silver Bough, a magical branch from an Elm tree. The second is for those that are gifted with The Sight, a unique vision of the Unseen world only available to certain ancient families and the third is the rarest of them all, by invitation. One of those will allow you to pass into the unseen world.'

'And you truly believe all of this?' asked Joe in a disbelieving voice. The old man was talking nonsense. 'You really think there is a silver Elm tree somewhere or that some people can see things that aren't really there! And I suppose a Pixie is going to walk up to someone and just give them an invitation for you to go to their birthday party.'

The old man stood up, a look of fury had passed over his face fuelled by Joe's words.

'You do not have time to mock me young man, Peter is in danger. Don't be blinded by the things that you can see. There is much more to this world than what is in front of your eyes. You cannot see the air but you know it is there. You cannot see love, or sadness but you feel them inside you. Have you ever lost something that you were certain about where you left it?'

'Careless mistakes,' replied Joe back to the old man, dismissing the argument he was putting forward.

'Well what about the pretend friend you had when you were a young child. That was real wasn't it?'

'At the time it was, but he was probably just in my imagination. No adults could see him.'

'That's because their eyes are blind to things their brains don't understand. What about when you see something out of the corner of your eye, but when you looked there was nothing there? The unseen world does exist and Peter was one of those who possessed The Sight, he could see things that no one else could.' The old man paused, watching Joe thoughtfully, wondering if he was going to make a run for it. 'But now you're quiet. Have you nothing to say to that, does it not surprise you?'

'We all just thought he was talking to himself,' said Joe thinking about what Peter was like at school.

'Peter has The Sight as did his grandmother before him. He would have been talking to things he saw, small creatures like Sprites, things you wouldn't be able to see yourself,' explained the old man, slightly calmer now as he felt that Joe was starting to believe him.

'How do you know all of this?' asked Joe, part of his brain still told him to run and come back for his bike another time, but another part was becoming curious to know more.

'My name is Sir Edgar Gorlois, Duke of Tintagel and one of the original members of The League of White Knights,' he gave a low bow as he introduced himself before continuing. 'We are an ancient group of Knights founded by King Arthur himself to protect the human world from the dangers of the unseen world. After Gawain and Belphoebe suffered their fate here by the hand of Morgan Le Fay, a Faerie Sorceress and their Queen, Arthur swore to protect England forever and left a band of four knights to remain hidden but protecting all known entrances like this one, keeping the Silver Bough safe and watching over the families with The Sight.'

Edgar now started to walk into the centre of the circle nearer to Joe. Although Joe was still unsure about the old man, he stayed where he was alongside Gawain's stone.

'You may have heard the old tale about King Arthur coming back to save England in its time of greatest need,' continued Edgar, Joe nodded. 'Well, he won't be coming back because he's never left. In me I carry his beliefs and ideals and am here to serve England and prevent creatures from the underworld from entering this world again.'

'But that would mean you were thousands of years old!' Joe replied with a laugh.

'About 1500 years old actually, but I loose track from time to time. My body is not a day older than when the Immortalitus spell was performed on us by Arthur's friend and teacher Merlin.'

'So where are the other three Knights?' asked Joe.

'Unfortunately they are all dead. There is now only myself left. We can still be killed just like anyone else, still be affected by viruses or have our bodies harmed, but every cell that makes us up remains the same and never ages. I was an old man when I became a White Knight as I am today, but despite my appearance, I have the strength of a man much younger.'

'Then why do you carry a stick?'

'For appearances sake. If I look old, I must be old. That way I don't draw attention to myself and no one takes any notice of me. But I have been amongst you and your families for many years. I swore to watch over those with The Sight and came to Parsley Bottom when Peter moved here.'

'Peter's mum knows you watch her family. The police are probably looking for you; they think you may have something to do with Peter's disappearance.'

Sir Edgar frowned, 'then we need to move fast. I too want to find Peter, but if he entered the unseen world his life is in danger.'

'From what?'

'From creatures you could never imagine. He could be killed,' Edgar explained with no emotion. 'Or worse than that.'

'What could be worse than being dead?' asked Joe with a laugh

'The Faerie Queen may realise how useful Peter could be and use him to show her the way into the human world which she wants to rule for herself and then we would all be doomed.'

'So if the Faeries can't get into this world, how do those small creatures that Peter talks to get to be here? Do they go between the worlds?'

'Sprites are small creatures that live in both worlds but don't cross between the two. The ones that Peter talks to have probably lived here for a long time, and more likely been friends to Peter since he was a child. Maybe they were Peter's imaginary friends?'

'So can't we just go in and take him out of the unseen world?' said Joe.

'It's not that easy I'm afraid. I don't know how to get in. Peter is the only child of the last living line of families that posses The Sight. Without him we can't see the entrance.'

'What about his grandmother? You said she had The Sight before Peter,' said Joe desperately trying to think of a way to get Peter back.

'She does but age has blinded her and she can no longer see anything but blurred clouded shapes.'

'What about the silver twig you mentioned.'

'The Silver Bough. There are only clues as to its whereabouts, but so far no one has found it. My brother, the Earl of Rosslyn, who was also one of the White Knights, was the sacred guardian of the Silver Bough and he too died last year. His tomb is held in the vaults beneath Edinburgh Castle'

Joe wandered aimlessly around the large stones, kicking at the loose gravel around his feet. He still couldn't quite believe what Edgar was telling him, it was a tale of fantasy and imagination, but some of what he said about Peter seemed to make sense.

He looked over to Edgar, who stood watching him whilst he leant on his twisted stick. The daylight glinted in his silver beard.

'Can you prove anything you've said?' asked Joe finally.

Sir Edgar nodded his head.

'Meet me at the graveyard in one hour and I will show you. Bring your friends too, I will need your help if we are to stand any chance of getting Peter back,' with that the old knight turned his back on Joe and walked towards the outside of the circle, leaving him a clear route to his bike and his way out.

12. THE BOX OF ROCKS

Steven had arranged for Georgia to meet him outside the pub where she had dropped him the evening before. She drove over to the house of Mr McRae, the man who had found the original meteorite, who lived in an old water mill on the outskirts of town, then she waited in the car.

The building was old, the roof sagged in places and the white paint on the wood panelled sides was blistering and peeling off. The half submerged wheel of the water mill didn't look like it had been used for some time from the amount of plants and mosses that were growing in the crevices between the wooden paddles.

Steven knocked loudly on the glass of the side entrance door and waited for someone to come. Eventually the round figure of an elderly woman wearing a bright floral patterned dress with a faded apron over the top came to the door and opened it slightly. Her thinning hair was wound in tight curls and the circular glasses that balanced on top of her two red cheeks looked like they were floating in mid air.

'Good morning Mrs McRae, I'm Steven Knight, from the National Meteorite Society,' he lied. 'I wonder if I could ask a few questions about the meteorite that you found?' He had been thinking about what to say before he arrived and decided it would be better not to tell the McRaes anything about the bacteria.

'You better talk to my husband,' she replied grumpily as she opened the door wider and moved aside to let him in. 'He's out in his greenhouse as usual,' she pointed through the kitchen to the back door then walked slowly back into the lounge; Steven had obviously disturbed her daytime television viewing.

'And tell him he needs to clean out the dishwasher!' she shouted from the other room.

Steven left the kitchen, which smelt strongly of cat food, and crossed a bit of wooden decking over the last section of river water to a secret garden behind the mill on the northern side of the river. The lawn was perfectly cut and beautifully flat and it was surrounded by densely packed borders of coloured flowers. There were small sections of rocks with tiny plants growing out of every crevice and benches placed at carefully chosen positions to get the best views. As Steven walked onto the grass he could see the top of the greenhouse pointing up above an old stone wall, so headed in that direction. In the middle of the wall was an archway with an old twisted plant growing around it. From its leaves hung small pale blue flowers that gave off a sweet smell as Steven walked beneath them.

Inside the greenhouse, Steven could see the shape of an elderly man standing over rows of black trays, pushing seeds deep into the compost then patting them gently down. He looked up, saw Steven and gave a friendly wave, despite not knowing who Steven was; very different to his wife. His smiling face had some colour in it, probably from spending so much time in his garden.

'Good morning Sir,' shouted Mr McRae from inside the greenhouse, 'come on in.' He slid one of the glass doors across to let Steven in.

'I'm Steven Knight from the National Meteorite Society,' lied Steven once again as he held his hand out, 'you must be Mr McRae?'

'Call me George,' he replied shaking Steven's hand. 'I suppose you're here about the Meteorite I found then are you?'

Steven nodded as he looked around at the homemade wooden shelves and the rows of seed trays lined up on them. He could feel the warm damp air inside the greenhouse already making his forehead sweat.

'Well, if you look above your head you'll see where it came in,' instructed Mr McRae in a Scottish accent.

Steven looked up to a window in the roof of the greenhouse that was now patched up by a plastic carrier bag and some parcel tape where something had obviously come through.

'It happened a couple of months ago. I was lying in my bed reading when I heard that glass break. Thought it might be kids at first, so I came out to have a look but there was no one here at all. Saw a few lights in the sky but nothing else. Next morning I saw a big rock sitting on the floor there, cracked in two. It even chipped my paving slab. From what it looked like in the middle, it didn't look like a normal stone so I took it over to a friend of mine at the museum in Harrogate for him to take a look. Said it was a meteor from the shower we had. I've found some others since.'

Steven was already familiar with the story of discovery, but Mr McRae's last words made him look up with surprise.

'Other meteorites? How many?' He asked.

'I dunno, not counted them, but I put them in a box in my shed. When you know what you're looking for you find the little rascals everywhere. Nearly broke the blades on my lawnmower a few times. Found some others in my flower beds. Even found a couple in the algae when I was clearing out around the edge of the river.'

'Would you mind if I had a look at them please George?' Sir Adam would be pleased with Steven for finding these other examples, even if they didn't contain the same bacteria as the original one.

'You can take them away with you if you like. I noticed they must have metal in them, magnets stick to them you know?' He wiped his hands on a dirty towel and walked out of the greenhouse followed by Steven. At the far end of the garden tucked away behind some trees in a more shaded area was the shed.

Steven stood and waited patiently outside as there was obviously not enough room in the shed for the both of them. After several seconds a voice from inside said, 'here we are,' and Mr McRae came out carrying a shoe box with a bent lid. They sat on one of the benches and opened the box. Inside were five meteorites all of differing sizes but similar in colour to the one Steven had seen inside MI6. After a brief look at the box of rocks, he could tell that none of them were split open which reassured him that if there was bacteria in these rocks it was contained within. As Steven examined one in his hand he realised that there wasn't much difference from a normal rock except for the flecks of iron on the crusted surface and the fact that it was heavier. Steven knew that he would have to get these samples back to MI6 for testing to see if they contained the same bacteria as the original one.

Thinking of the next part of his investigation, Steven turned his attention away from the box of meteorites sitting on his lap.

'Who owns the land around yours?' asked Steven.

'It's mainly public land, there are footpaths criss-crossing all over it. Beyond that is Baxley Farm. Richard Baxley mainly has cows, famous for it round here he is. There's a small lay-by further up the road where walkers leave their cars if you want to have a look over there?'

They both stood up and Steven started to talk to Mr McRae about the plants and flowers in his garden just to be polite, but soon they were disturbed by the loud voice of Mrs McRae calling her husband inside to start on a list of jobs that needed to be done.

As he walked through the kitchen Steven lifted the box of meteorites up and said, 'Thanks for these. If you find any more, I'm staying at the Fox and Hound Pub in town for a few days.' With that they parted and Steven went and sat in the passenger seat of the car.

Whilst Georgia started the engine Steven opened the box again and started to take another look at the meteorites.

'Have we got a metal detector?' he asked her.

13. PROOF OF IDENTITY

An hour later Joe met Max and Scarlet at the tree top platform in the woodland overlooking the river that the three of them had visited the day before. He had told them both of how the symbol took him to the Faerie Ring and about the conversation he had had with Sir Edgar.

'It seems a bit far fetched to me,' said Max.

'What's happening now,' Joe asked Scarlet who had the binoculars trained on the graveyard as well as the church. When they arrived there was already a police car parked on the verge outside the church so they had decided to continue straight to the hideout in the woods.

'Any sign of Sir Edgar yet?'

'No. Hang on. I think I've got him. He's hidden in the undergrowth on the opposite side of the road. The brown suit he wears camouflages him well.'

'Let me see,' Joe took the binoculars from Scarlet, 'yes that's him.'

'If he's got nothing to hide, why doesn't he just go up to the police and tell them what he told you?' said Max.

'If we are having trouble believing him, I don't think anyone else will either,' replied Joe. 'Wait, he's walking away now towards town.'

A policeman was unrolling a tape between two posts as a sign to prevent anyone from entering the graveyard. He didn't seem to take any notice of the old man as he walked past leaning on his stick.

Nothing else happened until two figures emerged from the church. 'That looks like your dad,' Max said to Joe, 'who's that woman he's talking to.'

Joe refocused the binoculars towards the entrance of the church where his father and a woman were talking. It looked like she was crying.

'It must be Peter's mum. There are also some other policemen taking samples of the slime from the blanket and it looks like Mrs Merchant is not very happy about all these things happening in the church.'

'Good day to you all,' came the polite voice of Sir Edgar as it appeared in the hole beside the tree trunk.

Both Scarlet and Max gave a little squeak in surprise as they stared at the old man as he nimbly lifted himself through the hole and sat on the platform with the children. They all shuffled away from him slightly, still unsure whether they trusted him yet, but there wasn't anywhere to go apart from over the edge of the platform.

'I thought you had called the police when I saw them in the graveyard,' he said to Joe, 'but then I spotted the light reflecting off the lens of your binoculars from up here. I presume our friend has updated the two of you on what we talked about earlier.'

Scarlet and Max both nodded together at the same time.

'Good, well you wanted proof and I have it for you. All I can do is put the facts before you and let you make up your own minds,' continued Edgar as he removed a metal tube from his jacket. He unscrewed the top from the tube and placed a roll of coarse yellow cloth in front of them, gently untying the string around it and carefully opening it out. Inside the cloth were several pieces of yellow brown paper, the edges worn and soft with age and slightly torn in places. All three of the children stared down at the top paper. There was an ornate border of entwined coloured patterns around a block of writing that none of them could understand. At the top of the paper was a large unrecognisable letter similar to the writing that Joe had already seen inscribed on the stones at The Faerie Ring. This letter gleamed with gold still polished and shiny, despite the dullness of the paper it was drawn on. At the bottom of the page a thick red waxy circle was indented with a shield containing three crowns within.

'This is the Order to Service from King Arthur to myself,' Edgar traced some of the letters with his finger as he talked, 'asking for my trust and loyalty to protect England with my life. At the bottom here,' this time he pointed at the red wax, 'is where Arthur Pendragon's ring was impressed into the wax.'

They all peered over the sheet of paper, not daring to touch it in case it should disintegrate. Edgar carefully lifted it like it was a newborn baby, to rest safely by his side. The second piece of paper looked like it had a drawing of a complex tree with branches and leaves around the outside, but within its branches were small names joined together by fine lines.

'This is the Shipley family tree,' explained Edgar. 'The surnames have changed over the years as different generations of children married into other families, but here you can see your friend Peter Crisp, his parents and grandparents and so on. Those with a flower next to their names are those that have the gift of The Sight. All of the family have died out over the years except on Peter's side and he is the last. My fellow Knights and I have watched over every one of them during their lifetime.'

Edgar turned the piece of paper around so that his audience could all see clearly what he was talking about before continuing. 'We all had a part of the family to look after, but my brother Sir Hadwyn, Earl of Rosslyn, the bravest and purest of the four, also had charge of the Silver Bough.'

'These papers all look impressive but anyone could have made these or bought them from somewhere, and we can't even read what that says,' said Max bravely pointing to the paper with the wax seal on, 'so we still don't know if you're telling us the truth and we still don't know where Peter is.'

'This is true,' replied Edgar patiently, 'but maybe these will help convince you of my age and then, maybe you will believe the rest of what I say to be true.'

Sir Edgar now carefully lifted the family tree so that it was resting on top of the Order to Service to reveal some smaller pieces of paper. Edgar picked up the first piece and passed it to Joe who was sitting to his right.

'This is a copy of a page taken from an ancient book called Historia Brittonum which was written over one thousand years ago. It means "The History of the Britons" and in Chapter 56 the twelve battles of King Arthur are documented along with the names of the Knights of the Round Table as well as myself, Edgar Gorlois, Duke of Tintagel.' Although the writing appeared slightly different to normal English, Joe could make out the letters that made up Edgar's name amongst the rest of the text.

'Are there any pictures of you with Arthur?' asked Scarlet, trying to think of a way to convince both herself and Joe.

'No,' replied Edgar shaking his head. 'Any illustrations showing King Arthur were done at a later date after he was dead and were based on the imagination of the illustrator and not fact. But, you may find this helps you believe what I say.' Edgar passed an old photograph to Max, 'this is an old photograph of all the staff at the Rolls Royce factory in Derby in 1908. I worked there until 1914 and if you look on the back row you can see me. Even if you don't believe that I was alive in King Arthur's time, you must agree that if that was me in 1908 I would certainly be dead by now.'

Max looked carefully at the picture. It was a brown photograph with one or two black spots on it and showed a group of men; the front row, who were obviously more senior, sat on chairs in their best suits with top hats, whilst the rest of the workers stood behind wearing identical brown suits, shirts and ties. At the back on the right hand side of the picture was a man with a short grey beard which Max had to admit looked a lot like Sir Edgar. He stood tall and stiff, looking directly at the camera and didn't appear to be any different to the man that was sat in front of them.

'It really does look like you!' said Scarlet who had been looking over Max's shoulder. Max remained silent.

Edgar passed another photograph to Scarlet. 'This is me in the Home Guard in 1942 during the second World War. I was too old to join the regular army so volunteered for the Home Guard ready to defend Britain in case of invasion by Germany.'

Scarlet examined the photograph closely scanning the three rows of soldiers in their uniforms until she came across the now familiar face. Standing once again at the back was Edgar but this time he was clean shaven but there was still the sharp intense look in his eyes as he stared out of the black and white photograph from beneath his cloth cap.

'You must admit it Max, there's no way he could have been in those photographs on those dates unless he was actually there, Edgar could be who he says he is' said Joe to his friend.

'Maybe,' was all Max would say.

'If he's telling the truth about his age, he has no reason to lie to us about Faeries and the unseen world. If my believing Edgar can do something to help find Peter, then I'm willing to take a chance,' said Joe defiantly.

'I want to help too,' said Scarlet.

There was silence from Max. They all looked at him, his head down not wishing to look any of them in the eye. 'Alright,' he grudgingly said. 'I'll do it,' he agreed, still unconvinced, 'but how do you think we can find him, especially if he really has gone into another world.'

'Edgar said that the only way to get into the unseen world is by having The Sight, the Silver Bough or an invitation, so the only real way for us to gain access is to find the Silver Bough and go through the portal to bring Peter back.'

'Can't we get someone else to do it, like the army or something?' said Max trying to think of excuses.

'They won't believe us,' Joe said, 'and we can probably get in without being noticed whereas an army wouldn't be able to do that.'

Sir Edgar coughed politely trying to get the attention of Max and Joe. 'You're forgetting one important thing,' he said. 'We don't have the Silver Bough.'

'No, but your brother did,' replied Joe excitedly. 'You said that his remains are in a tomb beneath Edinburgh Castle. If he was sworn to protect the Silver Bough he would have either taken it to the grave with him or left some sort of instructions for its safe keeping. Think about what most people would do with something valuable if you were to die; you would leave a will or instructions for someone you trusted to keep it safe.'

'That's true,' said Scarlet as they all nodded.

'When did the other White Knights die?' Joe asked Edgar.

Edgar thought hard about Joe's question, trying to recall from the numerous volume of events stored inside his head the exact information. 'Sir Cenweard was the first to die in London back in 1665 from the Black Death and Sir Aldwyn was killed in 1832 by the sword of a highwayman in Surrey after he tried to defend a lady from being robbed. Sir Hadwyn died from Pneumonia during last year's cold Scottish winter.'

'So if Sir Hadwyn also knew about the deaths of the other knights, he would likely hide the thing he's been protecting all of his life. And if he knew that you Sir Edgar were the last surviving White Knight he may have left you instructions where to find the Silver Bough and continue what he started. We need to go to Edinburgh Castle.'

14. A GRUESOME DISCOVERY

After a quick visit to the local hardware store out of town, Steven and Georgia made their way to the lay-by that Mr McRae had mentioned. They pulled off the main road and onto a chalky surface that was roughly marked out in parking spaces. Georgia parked the car in a cloud of dust that had been kicked up by the tyres, beside two other cars that were already there. Beyond the wooden fence that separated the road from the grass and trees, a sign directed walkers across different public footpaths.

Opening the boot of the car Steven reached in and removed the metal detector from its packaging as well as a shiny new spade. Georgia lifted out a small square canvas box and lengthened the wide fabric strap so that she could carry it on her shoulder, then unfolded a map. Today Georgia had changed the brown suit for something more practical and wore a fleece and jeans together with a pair of trainers.

'Ready?' asked Steven.

As they walked through an opening in the fence and onto a well worn track which led into the woodland, Steven noticed a fourth car that crept slowly into the car park, there was something familiar about the driver and the suit he was wearing didn't look practical for walking or sightseeing. They crossed the river via a wooden bridge with no handrails, the thick bulrushes reached up high on both sides, hiding the water. A couple of serious walkers wearing boots and backpacks strode energetically in the opposite direction as they followed the path deeper into the woods to the land behind Mr McRae's property.

Once they were there they sat on a fallen tree trunk and began to plan their project.

'So, we are here,' said Georgia pointing to an area on the map. She marked a small cross onto the map with a red pen. 'If we walk through the woodland and start here,' she pointed to another spot and made a second cross, 'that is the boundary of the wood where it meets Mr McRae's land. If you swing the metal detector from side to side as you walk you should be able to cover a width of at least a meter.'

They picked their way off the footpath and into woodland that had not been trampled down by the heavy boots of numerous walkers. The small branches of trees also appeared to grow lower here and they would often have to duck slightly or snap them off to make their way through.

Georgia carefully navigated their way by constantly referring to her map as well as a small compass she carried in the palm of her hand. Once they had arrived at the point where the second cross was on Georgia's map Steven turned the metal detector on and began walking in a straight line. He swept the metal detector in front of him from one side to the other under the watchful eye of Georgia and her map, making sure that he continued in the right direction.

Occasionally a high pitched squeal would cut through the gentle hum made by the metal detector as it passed over a metallic object, but it uncovered nothing more significant than an old tin can or a few coins. Each time Steven walked up and down, Georgia marked it on the map and by the end of two hours they had found two other meteorites similar in size to the ones from Mr McRae's garden. They carefully stored them inside Georgia's canvas bag then decided to try a different section of woodland beside the river.

Once again they began searching in a methodical way, all the time referring back to the map. Whilst Steven started walking along the river edge swinging the detector from side to side, Georgia removed two clear plastic sample tubes from her bag and took them down to the river to take some water for testing. She knelt down at the edge of the river bank and leant forward. The thickness of the reeds and bulrushes in front of her hid the water below so she had to hold them apart with her other hand like she was parting hair. The water quickly filled the plastic tube. She tightly screwed the top on then held it up to the sky, looking at the little bits floating in the green coloured water.

She stood up and checked on Steven's progress before moving further up the river to take a second sample. As she parted the reeds she saw what looked like a soggy bundle of clothes slightly further out that must have become caught up in the reeds against the flow of water. She took her water sample as before then walked back towards the nearest tree and snapped a branch from it. Using the branch she reached out over the water and managed to hook it onto the bundle of clothes then leant backwards and began pulling using all of her body weight against the resistance of the wet clothes. Suddenly the clothing came away from the reeds and Georgia slipped backwards falling onto her back.

Amongst the reeds she was now staring at something more than just clothes.

A disfigured hand reached out of the water.

At first she was confused. The hand looked larger than she thought it should do, almost like it had sucked in lots of the river water and Georgia thought for a short moment that it was not real at all. The skin appeared white and waxy, but there were patches of it missing which revealed the grey-brown flesh beneath the skin. The edges of these missing patches were uneven and thicker, almost like it had been melted away to the fleshy meat beneath. As an operative assistant Georgia had never actually seen a dead body before, she was much more used to writing reports and doing research.

'Steven!' She said in a broken voice as she tried to take deep breaths of air into her lungs. She couldn't help but keep staring at the hand and its ghostly white fingernails. It grasped at the air, fixed in a disfigured grip like the hooked talons of an eagle clawing at its prey.

'Steven!' Georgia said once again more desperately without looking round.

'What is it?' he asked casually as he strolled up beside her. 'Have you found another meteorite?'

Georgia pointed a shaking finger towards the river. Steven followed the direction she was pointing in and saw the hand reaching out of the water. A cold shiver went through his body followed by a wave of sickness as his stomach tightened, but his mind stayed alert and soon instructed his body what it needed to do. He pulled a mobile phone from his pocket and called the police immediately then helped Georgia onto her feet and slowly moved her further up the bank out of sight of the hand. He sat down closely next to Georgia, put his arm around her still shaking shoulders and waited for the police to arrive.

15. UNLOCKING THE KEY

That afternoon Sir Edgar and the children arrived on the train to a rain soaked Edinburgh. The sky was dark grey and the damp clung to their clothes making them feel cold and heavy to wear. Each of the children had told the same lie to their parents that they were going to stay over at a friend's house that night but had secretly agreed to meet up with Edgar at the local train station to get the connection to Harrogate then on to Edinburgh.

They spotted Edinburgh castle high up on the hill as the train approached Waverley Station and now they stood waiting to get in along with the other tourists. Once they had their tickets they walked across a bridge and through a tall gatehouse with two rigid stone statues standing guard either side of the entrance. The stone walls of the castle appeared grey and black, soaked by the rain water which also made some of the well worn flagstones smooth and slippery to walk on.

They continued to walk up a grey stone slope with the walls high around them making them feel like they were walking along a small street through an old town. Ahead they could see another archway to walk through which seemed to form the foundations to a house.

'Wait here,' said Edgar and he dashed through a red door without any explanation.

The children stood to the side of the walkway feeling slightly nervous about suddenly being left on their own in such an unfamiliar place. The other tourists walked slowly past them pointing at the different parts of the castle as they went. Max couldn't help but feel guilty that he was here without his parent's permission and the inside of his stomach felt like a tight knot. He hadn't been able to eat any lunch and was beginning to feel sick.

Suddenly Edgar came out of the red door with a guide book in his hands.

'Won't get far without this,' he said cheerfully opening it to a map of the castle.

'Haven't you been here before then?' asked Joe as they continued towards the next gate.

'Yes, just the once, but that was in 1566,' one of the tourists turned round and looked disbelievingly at Edgar who seemed oblivious to their stares and continued. 'My brother had been working as a Captain in the Scottish Royal Guard for Queen Marie de Guise until her death in 1560. He then continued under the employment of her daughter, Mary Queen of Scots who seemed to look favourably on Hadwyn and promoted him to Major. This allowed him certain freedom and privileges with Mary and at the birth of her son James in 1566 he was allowed to invite me to join in the celebrations held here inside the Royal Palace.'

They continued to walk through the stone archway and underneath a metal portcullis which, when lowered, would have kept out any invading force, but today allowed the friendly tourists to roam freely about the castle grounds. As they came through the dark tunnel and into the light again, the area opened up to reveal a series of black guns pointing out of small gaps in the thick stone wall and over the castle bank below.

'It's all changed so much since that time,' continued Edgar thoughtfully. 'It was a working castle back then. Around here lots of soldiers would be parading and practising at regular intervals. Even sheep and pigs would be running round freely and if you didn't see them, you could certainly smell them. It was like a small enclosed town, self sufficient and heavily protected.'

A loud bang unexpectedly ripped through the air in front of them, followed by a plume of white smoke which looked bright and clean in comparison to the grey clouds that hovered low around the castle. They all instinctively reached up to protect their ears from the noise, but there were no further explosions. Ahead they could see the long black barrel of the gun that had just been fired.

'Who are they shooting at?' asked Max nervously.

'That's one thing that hasn't changed,' Edgar exclaimed excitedly. 'It's called the One o'clock gun and it's fired every day at one and has done since Mary's days. It's sort of like a clock so that ships in the Firth of Forth knew what time it was.'

Edgar passed some sandwiches round whilst they stood looking at the view over the roof tops of Edinburgh which was limited because of the weather. After a few minutes Edgar was eager to continue.

'Next stop is Saint Margaret's Chapel, just up there,' he said pointing up a grass bank where grey rocks poked out from within.

They all followed Edgar along the shiny grey stone surface as it curved upwards and under yet another archway. As they entered an open area, ahead of them they could see a very plain square stone building with a name plate telling them that this was Saint Margaret's Chapel.

Edgar strode through the doorway followed closely by the three children. Inside was just one room. The chapel walls were all painted white and there were small wooden seats running along both sides of the outer walls. At the far end was a separate section through a stone archway that was supported by carved pillars. The table beyond the arch was covered with an ornate purple and cream coloured cloth and a small stained glass window cast what little light it could into the chapel, relying on modern day electrical lighting to see clearly. Inside, a group of American tourists were admiring the stained glass at the far end whilst Edgar and the children waited patiently around the doorway.

'Is this where Hadwyn's tomb is?' whispered Max to Edgar, hoping that the day would end soon and he could get back to Parsley Bottom before anyone noticed he wasn't where he should be.

'No,' replied Edgar as if Max should have known better, 'this is where the key to Hadwyn's tomb is kept.'

Edgar pretended to be studying the roof inside the chapel whilst he waited for the Americans to leave. Eventually they made their way to the doorway and exited the building leaving Edgar and the children alone.

'You two stand next to the door and let me know if anyone comes in this direction,' Edgar instructed to Max and Scarlet as he moved further down the chapel towards the archway. Joe watched as Edgar lifted one of the small wooden benches and positioned it beneath the centre of the arch at the far end. Standing on top of the bench he was now tracing his fingertips along the zigzag pattern that was carved in the arch and counting quietly under his breath. Reaching into his trouser pocket he removed a small penknife and began to scratch away some of the dirt and cement from underneath one of the sections. After a very short amount of time the sound of the knife scraping on the stone beneath changed as the blade slid deeper between two flat surfaces.

Edgar let out a laugh of relief which echoed inside the chapel. Joe stood directly beneath Edgar and was watching closely.

'What are you doing?' asked Joe.

Edgar looked down to Joe, then across to the door where Max and Scarlet were standing, but neither of them were watching out for tourists, they had been curious to watch Edgar too.

'Keep watch. We can't have anyone coming in while I retrieve the key,' he instructed to his two guards at the door.

To Joe he said: 'Twenty five is an important number relating to King Arthur. In Winchester Castle hangs a wooden table painted with the names of the twenty five knights from King Arthur's court, you may know it as the Round Table. In order to retrieve the key I need to press the correct stones to release a hidden drawer.'

Edgar pointed at the pattern that joined one side of the arch to the other then continued to scratch a groove all around the stone he had already started until the blade slid freely all the way around it.

'This stone represents the twenty five knights that stood on the right side of King Arthur. We also need the ninth stone from the left,' explained Edgar as he counted across from the left hand side. 'King Arthur was one of the "Nine Valiants." These were a group of nine figures who best demonstrated the values of chivalry and became role models for all medieval knights. The Nine Valiants can be seen in paintings and tapestries, and even in the Houses of Parliament in London.'

'What were the values of chivalry?'

'Being a good Knight is about showing mercy and courage and protecting the innocent, the weak and the poor. You should be prepared to give your life for another and be the champion for good against all evils. They must also be gentle and gracious to women. But what truly makes a Knight is what's inside you here.' Edgar stopped scratching at the stone work and reached down and placed a hand on Joe's chest. Joe could feel his heart thumping as well as the heat radiating from Edgar's hand through his shirt.

'When the time comes, you will understand exactly what is inside you,' Edgar whispered.

'Quick!' said Scarlet from the door. 'Some people are coming this way!'

Edgar hadn't taken his eyes off Joe and as he removed his hand from his chest he nodded slightly. Joe began to wonder what Edgar knew about him.

Swiftly, Edgar jumped down from the wooden bench and bowed his head in prayer just as a tour guide led a group of visitors through the chapel door. All that the tourists saw was an elderly man sat on a bench, too old and frail to kneel on the floor, silently in prayer with a young boy beside him doing the same. None of the group thought there was anything unusual in the scene as the tour guide continued his explanation about the history of the building, never noticing that a couple of stones in the archway above their heads now appeared looser than the rest.

Waiting patiently, Edgar remained in the same position even as the group of tourists stood behind him looking through to the stained glass window beyond. As soon as they had left the building he jumped back on the bench and continued scraping away at the ninth stone. As the blade inserted itself around the stone triangle Joe could see that the stone had now become loose.

'Ready?' said Edgar to Joe with a wink.

Joe nodded whilst holding his breath at the same time. Edgar reached out and placed his left hand on the ninth stone and the right on the twenty fifth and pushed them both into the archway. The stones slid in with a hard dry grinding noise, a slight low vibration rumbled through the archway and in the second tier of stones a darker keystone clicked out slightly further than the rest as if released by a spring. Edgar grasped the stone and pulled it out further then reached inside. He then pushed the keystone back into place and the other two stones returned back to their original position.

He stepped down off the bench and opened his hand for Joe to look at the key. In the palm of his hand was an aged silver pocket watch, slightly scratched and dull in colour, even the hands of the watch didn't appear to be moving and were stuck at five o'clock. Joe looked at Edgar with confusion. He thought they were finding the key to Hadwyn's tomb, but instead they had a watch.

Edgar quickly closed his hand and put the watch into his pocket whilst smiling at Joe.

16. SIR HAWDYN'S INSCRIPTION

Sir Edgar and the children left Saint Margaret's Chapel and walked back the way they had come, through the small archway and round beside the Military Prison. As they went through the doorway they waited for a few seconds to give their eyes time to adjust to the darkness inside.

As they descended the stone steps they could feel the temperature getting colder as they went further down into the rock beneath the castle. The stone walls got damper the lower they went and were lit by electric lights shining against the rock causing green algae to form. At the bottom of the steps, they walked along a narrow passage. The children couldn't see past Edgar who was at the front of the procession so they all followed as closely as they could without tripping each other up. Apart from the sound of their shoes sliding over the grainy floor, they couldn't hear any other tourists in this part of the castle as it was not part of the official tour.

Edgar held his hand up to stop the children from walking into the back of him. He had stopped at a rusty iron gate that prevented anyone from going any further. Hanging across the bolt that drove into the wall was a modern looking lock, holding it securely closed. Edgar picked it up in his hands and examined it.

'Won't your pocket watch open this then,' said Max sarcastically.

'Can I borrow your pen knife,' Joe asked Edgar as he looked at the rusted hinges fastened into the damp stone. Edgar passed it to him and with a little persuasion from the knife; Joe managed to loosen the pins from the barrel of the hinge so that Edgar could lift the gate and move it out of their way.

They continued along the passage once again. On the right they passed a series of rooms one of which Max managed to look inside. It appeared to be a plain square room with a curved roof and a wooden frame along the side wall from which hung several hammocks.

'This leads to the vaults underneath the castle,' explained Edgar. 'They've been used in the past for many different reasons. Merchants stored wine and goods here, some families lived in them at times and they have even been used as a soldier's barracks and a prison at one time.'

The corridor appeared to be getting narrower as well as lower in height as they continued along it. There was no electrical lighting in this part of the vault and Edgar was relying on the light from the torch that he carried in front of him. Because of his height Edgar permanently held his head lower and kept ducking as they passed beneath thick stone arches.

Eventually they came to a circular chamber where two other passageways met with the one they had just come down. Here they could all stand upright as the ceiling was a lot higher than in the other passageways; in fact, high above them, there appeared to be a shaft of daylight coming down towards them.

'We are directly under the Royal Palace,' said Edgar, noticing the children looking up.

The beam from the torch cast strange shapes and movements on the circular walls that surrounded them all. Edgar swung the torch towards the ground and started to kick away at the loose dust that covered the floor. At the entrance to one of the other passageways he found what he was looking for and was now kneeling on the floor brushing the dirt away with his fingers. The children crowded round to have a look.

'What's that?' asked Joe who noticed that there was a symbol carved into the large flat stone that marked the start to one of the other tunnels.

'It's King Arthur's crown and shows us the way to Sir Hadwyn's tomb. It's the same as the one I showed you from King Arthur's ring imprint that was in the wax seal on my Order to Service,' explained Edgar as he stood and walked through the archway and into the next passage.

The children followed without asking any more questions until they reached a perfectly round smooth surfaced stone that was fixed behind two thick but short columns of stone on both sides, blocking the passage.

'Maybe we took a wrong turn,' said Max with a nervous laugh.

Edgar was now examining the circular stone as closely as he had the floor at the entrance of the passage. In the centre was a small hole. He blew dust from the hole then reached into his pocket and retrieved the watch he had found in the chapel. Carefully he unscrewed the back of the watch and blew into the mechanism releasing a small white cloud of dust to sparkle in the light from the torch. Edgar licked his lips with anticipation, hoping that the key worked the way it should otherwise there would be no other way to get into the tomb. He then unscrewed the glass dome from the front of the watch. What he now held in his hands didn't truly resemble a pocket watch at all. There was a silver band of metal around the edge with blackened metal cogs and gears exposed behind the white enamelled clock face. The two silver hands pointed out at a fragile angle secured to the clock face by a thin metal pin. Edgar gently slid the skeleton of the watch into the hole at the centre of the stone until there was a very faint click.

'When the cogs at the back of the watch are put in the correct position they will activate the mechanism behind the stone,' Edgar whispered to the children. 'The twenty five Knights of the Round Table are represented by twenty five minutes or the number five on a clock face. Nine for the Nine Valiants for the hour hand.'

With his index finger he then carefully rotated the minute hand clockwise until it was on the number five, then the hour hand anticlockwise to the number nine. Then he held his breath.

Everyone stared at the circular stone and waited for something to happen.

At first there was a very faint clicking followed by a hissing sound like sand was draining into a container. Finally the stone started to rotate to the right and rumbled into the side of the passage wall to reveal the tomb's outer chamber. Directly ahead of them were two stone columns supporting a carved beam decorated with animals and writing. Beside the columns were two lions intricately carved into the white stone and appearing to support the weight of the beam on their clawed feet whilst surrounded by an assortment of serpents and mythical creatures winding their way around the borders and edges.

Edgar stepped into the chamber. The air smelt cold and stale and the breeze that he created by stepping onto the floor dislodged loose dust from the surface to swirl around his feet like mist on the sea. Edgar walked very carefully, checking everywhere he placed his feet, until he passed between the two columns.

In front of him was the tomb of Sir Hadwyn; a giant stone box with five figures carved into the side supported a life size stone carving of Sir Hadwyn, his hands peacefully resting on his chest with the hilt of his sword beneath. The blade continued down the centre of his body until it was hidden from view behind the shield which rested on his left side.

As the children entered the chamber from behind, Edgar knelt down to one knee and remained silent for a minute.

'Is this Sir Hadwyn?' asked Joe gently.

Edgar looked up and gave a nod of his head while Scarlet put a comforting arm around his shoulders. Max remained next to the stone columns feeling uncomfortable about being there.

'Look,' said Joe pointing at the five smaller knights on the stone box, 'one of these knights has your name engraved on it.'

Along the side of the box five knights stood with swords in their hands looking strong and brave. Beneath the feet of each knight was a carved name plate: Arthur, Ceneard, Aldwyn, Hadwyn, Edgar.

'King Arthur and The League of White Knights,' Edgar said proudly.

The figure of Arthur was different from the rest by the crown he wore as well as the more richly decorated armour, whilst the four white knights wore the same as each other, except for Edgar who held a shield in his left hand.

'Why are you the only one holding a shield?' asked Scarlet.

Edgar looked at the figures trying to work out why he was carved differently to the other knights.

'The shield must be relevant in some way,' said Joe, 'maybe Sir Hadwyn left you a clue.'

Joe leant over the top of the tomb and studied the figure of Sir Hadwyn and the large shield he held.

'Here!' said Joe excitedly, 'around the edge, there's a message. It looks like the same type of writing that's on the stones in the Faerie Ring,' Joe's voice echoed slightly inside the empty chamber.

Edgar stood up, looked over Joe's shoulder then began moving his finger along the pattern of letters whispering words to himself.

ᚠᚺᛖᚱᛖ ᚠᛚᛁᚷᚺᛏᛋ ᛟᚠ ᚨᚱᚱᛟᚹᛋ ᚲᛟᛗᛖ ᚺᛖᛞ ᛏᚠᚱᛟᛗ ᚨ ᚺᛖᛁᚷᚺᛏ
ᚨᚾᛞ ᛏᛖᚨᛗᚺᛋᛟ ᛚ ᛏᚱᛖᚲᛚᚨᚱᛖ ᛁᚺ ᚺᛁᛞᛞᛖᛋᚠᚱᛟᛗ ᛋᛁᚷᚺᛏ
ᚨᛗᛟᛁᚷᚺᛏ ᛏᚺᛖ ᛏᚺᛁᛚᛏᚱᛗᛋ ᚨᚾᛞ ᛚᛋᛞᛖᚱ ᛏᚺᛖ ᚲᚱᛟᚹᚾ
ᛏᚺᛖ ᛏᚱᚨᛋᛏᛖᛞᚨᚾᛞ ᚲᚨᚱᛖ ᛈᛁᛏᚺ ᚾᛖᚨᛞ ᛒᛟᚹᛖᚺ ᚺᛖᚹᚾ

ᛒᛚᛏᛟᛈ ᛏᚺᛖᛒᚱᛁᛞᚷᛖ ᚨ ᛞᛁᚲᛖᚱ ᚨᛏᛖᛁᛖ
ᛏᚺᛖᛒᚨᚾᛋ ᛚ ᛋᛈᛖᛖᛏ ᛋᚠᛁᚷ ᛏᚨᚱᛋᛚᛈᛖᛏᛖᚱ ᛏᛖᛚᛏᛖᛁᛖ
ᚠᚱᛟᛋ ᛖᛁᛖ ᛏᚱᛋᛗ ᛏᛖᛚᛚᛋ ᛏᚺᛖ ᛚᛏᛖᛁᛖᛈᛁᛚᛚ ᚲᚠᚱᛏ
ᛋᛁᚺᛖᛁᛋ ᛒᛖ ᛚᛋᛖᚺ ᛒᚨ ᛏᚺᛖᛒᚱ ᚠᚨᛖ ᚠᛏᚺᛖᚠᚱᛏ

He then reached inside his back pocket and passed Scarlet an old note book bound together by a strap of leather which was attached at one end to a pencil.

'Write this down for me,' he instructed to Scarlet who quickly unwound the note book and found a blank piece of paper.

'Where flights of arrows come down from a height,
And Stevenson's treasure is hidden from sight.
Amongst the thistles and under the crown
The trusted and pure with head bowed down

> Below the bridge, a piper alone,
> The bard's sweet song turns water to stone.
> From one true touch the stone will part
> And only be used by the brave at heart'

'But what does that mean,' asked Max. 'It doesn't sound much like a message to me.'

'It wasn't going to be easy to find the Silver Bough,' said Joe to Max. 'If it was, anyone would be able to find it. The message is a clue to wherever it's kept. Just think of the security Sir Hadwyn put in place to stop people getting into his tomb.'

Edgar stepped back from the tomb thinking of the words he had just retold to Scarlet. He wasn't sure what it all meant yet, but he knew that Hadwyn had left the message specifically for Edgar to find so that he could discover the location of the Silver Bough.

'We'd better go,' he said quietly as he bowed his head to show respect and thanks to his dead brother. Scarlet bound the note book up with the strap of leather and passed it back to Edgar, then they all walked back out of the chamber, between the pillars and stood once again at the circular stone entrance to the tomb.

Edgar reached to the pocket watch that could still be seen in the centre of the stone near to the wall, turned the hands back to the five o'clock position and the stone ground its way back to its original place. Once it had stopped moving, Edgar took the watch out of the hole, replaced the front and back and put it safely into his pocket.

As they walked back along the passage to the crossroads Edgar was silent with a sad look on his face, thinking about his brother and the riddle he had left them. This soon changed as he stopped abruptly and turned his head slightly towards the original passage they had come down so that he could hear more clearly. The children stopped too.

'What is it?' asked Joe in a nervous whisper.

'I thought I heard something,' replied Edgar quietly. They waited. Then they heard a squelching sound; like bubbles moving through a thick liquid and it seemed to be coming down the passageway ahead, directly towards them.

'This way,' said Edgar quickly changing direction and walking down the third passage.

'What do you think it is?' asked Max.

'It's probably what Peter saw in the graveyard and also what made him run to the Faerie Ring to escape' he replied. 'Come on, we can't stop. We all need to move quickly!'

17. THE THEFT

It felt like they had been sat on the river bank for the whole day, but it was in fact only about 10 minutes before they heard the siren of a police car and saw two policemen walked towards them. Georgia was glad that Steven had sat down next to her, her body desperately needed the reassurance of human contact and she found it comforting to feel his arm around her shoulders. Steven had become aware of a cold chill in his body, knowing that the dead person's hand was in the water just feet away from them. The shaking in Georgia's body had slowly stopped as she took more and more gulps of air and calmed herself down.

Steven stood up and walked over to meet the policemen and began explaining what had happened. From where she was, Georgia couldn't hear clearly what they were saying, but she noticed that they would occasionally turn and look at her or towards the hand in the water before continuing to talk. Other police officers began to arrive, some inspected the bullrushes whilst others sectioned off the area with yellow plastic tape and wrapped it from one tree trunk to another to prevent people wandering off the footpath to see what was happening.

Down by the river Steven could see other men putting on diving suits and walking into the water. An older man had now arrived and seemed to be directing some of the police officers around the arm then instructed them to bring it out of the water.

Steven and the policeman he had been talking to walked up towards Georgia.

'So you actually found the hand?' asked the Sergeant. Georgia stood up and nodded.

'I thought it was some clothes at first and tried hooking them out but then that, the hand. I must have dislodged it,' Georgia looked pale.

After taking some photographs, the hand was slowly lifted out of the water, dragging a ripped shirt behind it but without the body attached. Paper sheeting was then laid out on the grass and the arm was placed carefully on top of it, the older man then put on a pair of latex gloves and gently examined the hand, turning it over and lifting the shirt sleeve up.

Another policeman brought the metal detector that Steven had placed on the floor when Georgia called for him over for Sergeant Allen to see then whispered something into his ear.

'Is this yours?' Sergeant Allen asked.

'Yes, we had been looking in the woods for treasure,' Steven lied. He didn't know if he should tell the Sergeant the truth or not, but as soon as he said the word treasure he wished he hadn't. It wasn't a very good lie but he wasn't sure whether his superiors at MI6 would allow Steven to talk to the Police. Steven remembered what Seward had said in the white room that the information was "top secret and to be protected at all costs."

'Did you find any treasure?' asked Sergeant Allen sarcastically, who had not believed a word that Steven had said.

'No,' he replied shaking his head.

'What about the water samples you took?'

Steven hesitated for a moment, unsure what to say without making himself look suspicious; they had obviously looked inside the fabric bag and found the specimen tubes that Georgia had been filling. He decided to say what he could but without giving away any information.

'I need to speak to you in total confidence,' he said to Sergeant Allen in a whisper, who now looked confused. 'My name is Steven Knight and I work for MI6 in London.' Steven took his wallet from his inside jacket pocket and slid out his identity card for Sergeant Allen to look at.

'MI6? Why?' stuttered Sergeant Allen, 'What would you be doing here? Is this about Peter Crisp?' He handed the card back to Steven.

'I'm afraid I don't have clearance to tell you why I'm here, all I can say is that myself and my colleague are doing some field research in this area which we will need to continue doing for a few days and I need your total cooperation and discretion,' Steven said in his most authoritative voice. 'Who's Peter Crisp?' he added.

'He's a local boy. Went missing last night,' replied Sergeant Allen cautiously. 'That could be him,' he nodded towards the river and the hand that was now being carefully placed in a refrigerator box and packed with ice ready to be taken back to the Harrogate General Hospital for examination. 'He was reported missing this morning and hasn't been seen since. What do you mean by field research?'

'I'm afraid I'm not allowed to say.'

'You expect me to let you walk all over town without telling me what you are up to?' replied Sergeant Allen who clearly didn't like the thought of MI6 in Parsley Bottom.

'I expect you to cooperate with anything I ask, Sergeant Allen,' Steven replied once again trying to appear confident and authoritative. 'My superiors would be most unhappy to hear of any aggression or opposition from the local police force towards me and my *field research*.'

Although Sergeant Allen remained silent, he held back his displeasure at being pushed around by government officials from London.

The older man who had been examining the arm by the river walked up the bank towards Sergeant Allen. He was short with a full beard and spectacles that he seemed to prefer to peer over the top of rather than look through the lens.

'Mr Knight, this is Doctor Carter, the Home Office Pathologist from Harrogate,' said Sergeant Allen introducing Steven to the older man, trying to appear cooperative.

'If I could have a word please Sergeant,' asked the Pathologist, not wanting to talk in front of Steven.

'You can speak in front of Mr Knight. What have you found?'

'Very well. So far all we have is the left arm of a male, which is slightly swollen from being in the water but from the size of it I would say it looks too large to be the boy's and more likely to be that of a man, possibly over 40 years old. No identifying marks or jewellery. Some patches of hair so I should be able to get some DNA samples from them. There is quite a bit of dirt packed under the fingernails, some of which are broken consistent with clawing at the ground.'

'Is that all you've got,' asked Sergeant Allen.

'At the moment, yes. Once I've examined it more closely I will be able to tell you more,' there was a troubled look on the Pathologist face. 'Although, there is something strange. It looks like patches of the skin have been melted, almost like it's been dissolved in acid. The flesh below the skin looks like it's been eaten away but there are no teeth marks that I can see. Sometimes fish nibble away at flesh if its been in the water long enough to make it soft, but this looks like it may have only been in the water for a day, if that.'

Steven listened with great interest, remembering what Coldred had said about how the alien bacteria was acting in the same way as flesh eating bacteria. This could be relevant to Stevens's enquiries after all, especially as Sir Adam had said that they had already found traces of the bacteria in the river water.

'What about the crime scene, have the Underwater Search Team found anything else?' asked Sergeant Allen.

'Not yet. The divers are going along the river as well as both sides of the banks, but so far no sign of any other body parts. Because of the water current it's likely that the arm was washed down river from somewhere further up and the wet shirt got tangled on the bullrushes.'

'What do we have further upriver? The church, a few cottages and fields?' thought Sergeant Allen aloud.

'It depends on how far upriver you go. There is the industrial area towards the outskirts of town then farm lands and moors beyond that.'

'Where is the arm being taken?' asked Steven interrupting the two men.

Doctor Carter looked at Sergeant Allen for confirmation that he should answer, not knowing who Steven was or what authority he had to ask questions. Sergeant Allen frowned but reluctantly nodded his head for the Pathologist to answer.

'It's being taken to Harrogate General Hospital Mortuary where I will examine it more closely together with the Forensic Scientists. The Police station in Parsley Bottom is too small to handle things like this,' replied Doctor Carter, still cautious about Steven and his reasons for being there.

'I would like to see the report when it's complete if that's alright with you both. I will get my Commander to clear it at your headquarters in Harrogate. It could speed things up for you in identifying whose arm it is and may help you find that boy.' Steven tried to sound like he was helping the Sergeant, but really he wanted to see the report himself.

'So it may also be something to do with your *field research* then?' asked Sergeant Allen sarcastically.

'Possibly, but I'm not entirely sure,' replied Steven.

'I will leave the divers to keep looking around the scene whilst I go over to Harrogate with the arm. If they find anything else, please arrange to have it sent over to me immediately.' Doctor Carter walked back towards the river and discussed something else with some of the divers, directing them to search in other parts of the river before walking off in the direction of the car park with the chilled evidence box being carried by one of the policemen.

'Please can we go?' Georgia asked the Sergeant with a pleading look in her eyes.

'I suppose so, but I will need the name of your Commanding officer as well as the address of where you are staying.'

'Thank you,' Steven replied with a smile on his face. He didn't want to make an enemy of the local police force. 'I'm staying at the Fox and Hound if you need me for anything else and don't forget that I will need a copy of the Pathologist's report when you have it.'

Sergeant Allen picked up the metal detector and fabric bag containing the water samples and held them up for Steven to take, then escorted them towards the car park that was now overrun with police cars.

'Are you alright?' Steven asked Georgia, knowing she was still shocked by her discovery. 'I'll drive you home if you want.'

Georgia passed the keys to Steven who put the metal detector and the sample bag into the boot of the car. As he walked her round to the passenger door to open it for Georgia he noticed that it appeared to be open slightly. For a few seconds he thought he hadn't closed it properly when he had got out of the car, but when he saw the gap on the seat where he had put Mr McRae's box of meteorites, he realised that the car had been broken into and the meteorites had been stolen.

18. THE ESCAPE TUNNEL

Edgar led the children along the passageway, all the time listening to the sticky and wet sound that was coming from behind. Scarlet could feel the air inside the tunnel getting colder as it sloped down and away from the castle. Max wondered if Edgar knew where they were going and kept nervously looking over his shoulder to see if he could see what was following them, but every time he turned round he seemed to stumble. The paleness of his skin seemed to shine in the torchlight like the warm wax from a candle whilst the sound of his shaky and nervous breathing bounced loud and echoey in the enclosed tunnel.

Edgar flashed the torch rapidly from side to side, looking for alternative tunnels to dodge down, but all he could see was damp stone of endless tunnel. He didn't know when or where it would end, if it actually did, but all he could do was to keep running away from the sound behind them and try to lead the children to safety.

Suddenly they found the tunnel was blocked as they all ran directly into another iron gate. The torch fell from Edgar's hand and landed on the ground rolling forward beneath the gate and into the tunnel on the other side. As its beam of light spun round and round, it finally came to rest facing the ceiling above Edgar and the children. A light crumble of stone became dislodged from the wall the gate was bolted to and fell to their feet.

The noise continued to come behind them and very soon it would be on top of them.

'What do we do now!' shouted Scarlet panicking.

'It's like the other gate we got through,' said Joe rapidly as he noticed the rusted metal hinges that had absorbed the moisture from the rock. 'If we push it hard enough we should be able to get through.' With that he sat on the ground and began kicking at the rusted hinges as hard as he could.

The little light that shone in their direction, gave Edgar just enough visibility to be able to examine the lock. He took his penknife from his pocket and slid it into the key hole of the lock, wiggling it around a little trying to release the catch.

Nothing happened.

Behind them the bubbling sound seemed to be getting louder.

Max closed his eyes, not wanting to see what was coming towards them, whilst Joe continued to kick at the hinges, his head darting around as he kept glancing at Edgar's progress as well.

One of the hinges suddenly buckled under Joe's persistence, the brown and crumbly rust of the hinge twisting and snapping. Spurred on by Joe's success, Scarlet now joined him as he concentrated all effort on the second hinge.

Edgar tried twisting the knife slightly inside the lock as if it was a key, but it stayed closed. Frantically he wriggled it some more until finally there was a click, but he quickly realised that the click had come from the blade of the knife which had snapped and was now wedged inside the lock. There was no way the lock was going to be opened now, even if he had the key. Edgar turned away from the lock and started to concentrate on the hinges fixed on the wall.

'Joe! Edgar!' shouted Max as he began to see the outline of a dark shape coming towards them from further down the tunnel.

With one huge effort Edgar slammed his shoulder into the gate forcing the remaining screws to fall to the floor and the gate to spring back against the wall on the other side of the tunnel.

They all desperately scrambled through just as the dark shape emerged into the beam of torchlight that reflected off the tunnel walls.

Edgar leapt for the gate and pushed it back into position then forced his broken pen knife through one of the empty screw holes and into the stone wall with the heel of his hand until it was wedged stuck.

As soon as he withdrew his hand a blackened shapeless body slammed into the gate with a wet gurgling noise. The pen knife stayed in position holding the gate and preventing the creature from getting through. In the limited light they could make out a single cloudy white eye reflecting the limited light and staring back at them all through the iron bars. The creature let out a loud gurgling sound which sounded like air being forced through a wet tube.

Scarlet screamed, startled by the noise. She shuffled backwards on the floor trying to get as far away from the creature as possible.

Despite feeling scared, curiosity caused them all to remain sat on the floor on the other side of the gate staring at the unknown creature, amazed at what it actually was, but also feeling safer knowing there was a gate between them and it. It was a bit like looking at an animal in a zoo.

'We need to keep moving, the pen knife won't hold it for long,' said Edgar as he brushed the dirt from his trousers and retrieved the torch from the floor. He then started walking away from the gate.

'What is it?' asked Max as he gulped in air to help calm him down. There was even a little bit of colour coming back to his face.

'I don't know what it's called,' answered Edgar, 'but I think creatures similar to this were in the graveyard the night Peter stayed there. Now come on, we need to get out of here.' Edgar continued to encourage the children to leave, but they seemed transfixed by the creature.

'Look at the slime its releasing,' said Joe, 'It's like the slimy trail on the floor inside the church.'

Max took a step forward to take a better look at the black creature.

'Don't get too close,' shouted Edgar urgently to Max and pulled him backwards towards the rest of them.

'I've never seen anything like it before,' said Max. 'Is this a creature from the Unseen world?'

'No. Let's get out of here.'

'Maybe it's from the moon?' said Max jokingly. 'The eye certainly looks like a moon.'

Whilst they had been talking, the creature had done nothing but stare back at them. The long thin arms of the creature had extended from its body and the claw like fingers wrapped themselves around the bars of the gate. There were two extra long skeleton fingers at the end of each bony arm covered by a thin black skin stretched tight to the horny hook at the end. The creature poked a finger through the bars testing to see if it could reach any of the children, but all it did was claw at thin air.

'What's that smell?' asked Joe, raising his hand to shield his mouth.

Edgar noticed it at the same time and automatically covered his mouth and nose with the fabric of his jacket. There was now a sharp harsh smell in the tunnel that made the back of their throats sting. There was also a brown coloured smoke starting to appear around the creature where it pressed itself up against the gate.

'It's acid!' said Edgar. 'Come on, we have to keep moving. If the tunnel fills up with this gas it could kill us. This creature must be using acid to get through the gate. Come on, hurry!'

Panic set in once again and the children began running along the passageway trying to get as far away from the creature as possible.

The darkness swallowed them up once again as they headed into an unknown tunnel not knowing what would be front of them, but at least they now knew what it was that was following them. After several minutes of running in silence Edgar noticed that there was no sound of anything following them, so he slowed down to a quick walk, allowing the children chance to rest slightly.

'Where does this tunnel go?' Max asked the question everyone was thinking.

'I'm not entirely sure, but we've been moving constantly down hill and away from the castle. This could be one of the escape routes built into the castle rock in case it came under siege. Remember we went through that junction where three tunnels came together? Above it was the Royal Palace. Royalty could leave the castle undetected via underground passages. If this is one of them, it could lead to somewhere outside and below the castle'

Behind them a loud clang of metal echoed again and again off the sides of the tunnel walls. They all froze to the spot, realising that the creature had managed to get through the gate and was now inside the tunnel with them.

They started to run again.

Suddenly the passage came to a dead end. They were faced with a solid wall of stone with no where to go except back the way they had just come and straight into the path of the creature. Edgar frantically swung the torch light around them trying to find an exit, but they were trapped.

'There!' shouted Scarlet who had noticed that there no longer appeared to be a ceiling above their heads, 'we need to go upwards.' Edgar shone the light into a narrow tunnel that went upwards and into dark preventing them seeing to the top. There was a metal ladder fixed to one side of the tunnel. It was their only option.

'We have to climb,' Edgar said as he picked up Scarlet so that she could reach the bottom rung of the ladder, 'and we have to climb quickly. Go!'

As soon as one of the children had gone up several rungs of the ladder Edgar lifted another to start immediately after until there was just himself left in the tunnel alone. Once again he became aware of the damp bubbling sound in the tunnel getting closer and closer to him. The last of the children had cleared the bottom of the ladder so Edgar put the torch in between his teeth and put his hands on the bottom bar of the ladder and lifted himself up. He started to climb as quickly as he could and soon came to the feet of Max who was directly in front of him.

'Come on, keep moving as fast as you can,' Edgar said encouraging them on. He swung the torch up to shine above where the Scarlet was climbing at the front of the line. Above her, Edgar could see where the ladder finished and it looked like there was night sky above them.

'Keep going. Look above you, this takes us outside. I know your arms are probably hurting but we're almost there.'

He swung the torch back down beneath his feet and saw that the creature had now arrived at the dead end of the passageway. It looked up at the torch light then something very peculiar happened. It spread its arms out and a thin flap of skin unfolded from beneath its armpits like fine wings. It flapped hard pushing air beneath its body in swirls of dust, allowing it to rise off the ground.

'It's got wings!' said Edgar in surprise. He watched as the creature tried to fly up the tunnel, but it was too narrow, its wings kept hitting the side of the tunnel and causing it to slip back down. At one attempt though, as it fell backwards it managed to hook one long finger onto a rung of the ladder and hold on. Now it began pulling its body up the tunnel at an alarming speed.

Scarlet had now reached the top. She pushed her shoulder against a grate that covered the hole and lifted her weary body out onto wet grass. Joe followed closely behind her and they both sat there panting for breath as the head of Max also appeared above the hole.

Edgar's progress was delayed as he waited for the children to get out of the hole before him, but the creature had rapidly gained on them. Edgar shone the light back down the tunnel to see how far away the creature was and he realised that it had reached a part of the ladder that was only two rungs below his feet. He saw a thin clawed hand begin to reach up for his foot but as the light from the torch shone directly into its eye it seemed to retract back and almost squint in an attempt to shield its eye from the bright light. Edgar didn't need to wait for a better opportunity than this; he pulled one foot off a rung of the ladder and slammed it into the head area of the creature which then fell backwards down the tunnel.

Above him he noticed that Max had now managed to pull himself out of the tunnel allowing Edgar freedom to climb the rest of the ladder and lift his body out onto the grass beside the children. Never before had it felt so good to be lying on wet grass under a cold starry sky beneath the castle wall.

'Where are we now?' asked Joe.

'It looks like we have come up through the Castle Rock and this is probably Princess Street Gardens,' answered Edgar.

'There's no moon tonight,' said Scarlet as she stared up at the sky.

'Maybe that creature's eye really is the moon,' replied Max who lay beside Scarlet staring up into space, 'maybe it stole it from the sky. We could call it a Moon Stealer.'

The smile on his face soon turned to horror as a thin fingered hand reached up out of the tunnel hole and gripped Max around his ankle like a spiders legs contracting together. He was pulled with amazing strength towards the hole, despite Max clawing and grabbing at the slippery grass with his hands.

Suddenly there was a flash of brilliant white light that sliced through the air and separated the creatures arm from its body. Holding his sword firmly in both hands Edgar then leapt to the tunnel entrance and thrust it deep into the tunnel and into the eye of the Moon Stealer.

'Quick take off your trousers,' shouted Edgar to Max. Coloured acidic smoke had begun to drift from where the creature's hand remained frozen around Max's ankle.

Max seemed to be in shock and continued to stare at the creature's black skeletal hand that was still attached to him. Joe pulled at Max's shoes, prizing them from his feet then began rolling his trousers down. Using the fabric of the trousers to protect his hands he began prizing the creature's fingers apart whilst pulling at the trousers at the same time. Eventually it became looser and Max's ankle was free.

Edgar examined Max's ankle. Apart from the red marks where the fingers had been digging into his flesh, the material from his trousers appeared to have protected his skin from the acidic touch of the creature.

19. A RESTLESS KNIGHT

Max couldn't sleep much that night. The ankle that had been gripped by the creature was irritable even though the red finger marks had already begun to fade. He was grateful to Joe and Scarlet for getting the creature's hand off him, before it had caused any further damage, remembering how it had started to dissolve the metal gate with the acid it seemed to ooze. Although the skin was itchy, there was an odd numbness in the area too. Scarlet had found some Dock leaves in Princess Street Gardens to help soothe the inflammation, like she had done as a child whenever she had been stung by nettles. Later, Edgar had bought some Chamomile cream and rubbed it onto Max's ankle. The itchiness slowly began to ease and Max had fallen into a deep sleep.

After their encounter with the creature, Edgar had given Max his coat as it hung longer than his own so that it covered his bare legs. He then found an available room in the top floor of an old pub, consisting of no carpet, several mattresses on the floor and a single cream coloured wax candle for light. It hadn't cost much and the landlord didn't ask any questions about Max being slightly unclothed. The weather had got progressively worse. Heavy rain drops fell onto the roof drumming a constant rhythm while deep rumbles of thunder grumbled in the sky above like the scrape of heavy furniture moving across a wooden floor. Edgar had become quite protective of the children and sat watching them as they turned peacefully beneath their blankets. Part of him regretted bringing them with him on this quest, not truly knowing the dangers it would put them in. But, for all he knew, the dangers were no different to those Peter had found in Parsley Bottom. Certainly the slimy trail in the church and around Peter's blanket seemed similar to what they had seen from the creature in the tunnel.

Edgar had taken the opportunity to try and make some sense of Hadwyn's riddle by collecting as many of the tourist information leaflets from the entrance to the pub as he could carry. As he spread the leaflets out on the floor he continuously cross-checked what he was reading with the riddle Scarlet had written in his note book. Lying on the floor next to him was Ethera, the magical sword given to him by Nimue, The Priestess of Avalon. The indestructible white blade had earlier saved Max from the creature the children had nicknamed a Moon Stealer. As he knelt on the hard floor the candle light flickered in the draft that came up through the gaps between the floorboards and reflected sparkling dots of light like dancing glitter from the diamond dust imbedded in the metal blade.

The first leaflet that Edgar had started reading immediately caught his eye, it had the bold heading of "Arthur's Seat" written on the front and told the history of a group of hills to the east of Edinburgh. It mentioned in the leaflet that Arthur's Seat was thought to be one of the locations of King Arthur's castle, Camelot, however Edgar knew from his own experience that this was not true. Reading the leaflet further he came across an old Scottish name for the hill. They had called it "Àrd-na-Said," which they translated as meaning "Height of Arrows." Looking back at Hadwyn's riddle he re-read the beginning:

'Where flights of arrows come down from a height'

There were similarities between the Scottish name for Arthur's Seat and the wording of the first line in the riddle. Because the height at the top of Arthur's Seat was over 250 meters tall anything below that could be classed as 'down' from there. Edinburgh was the most obvious place the line was referring to so the Silver Bough could be hidden somewhere in the city. He read the second line:

'And Stevenson's treasure is hidden from sight.'

Edgar wondered what this could mean. They weren't looking for Stevenson's treasure. The Silver Bough had orginally belonged to a wise Druid called Arawyn Claremont so why, wondered Edgar, would his brother refer to someone else's treasure. He decided that the name Stevenson must have more relevance than it first appeared.

Although it was getting late, Edgar stayed up as long as his eyes would let him. He scanned through the remaining leaflets trying to understand more about the history and architechture of Edinburgh but in the end he couldn't give in to the tiredness that fell over him like a heavy blanket. He dreamt of the white eye staring out at him through a dark swirling mist, like black ink dispersing in water, before the eye consumed Edgar in a bright blinding light. The next thing he knew he was standing on the edge of a high rocky cliff, the wind whipping around and blowing his white hair, which appeared slightly longer than it was now, causing it to stick to the sweat on his face. Suddenly there was an empty weightless feeling like he was flying, but he was falling down along the cliff edge, the black stone passing quickly in a blur before he closed his eyes and waited to hit the bottom of the mountain. Then there was total darkness.

He awoke curled up like a baby on the hard floor, the leaflets all around him and despite the continuing damp weather, there was now daylight in the room.

Joe and Scarlet were standing beside Edgar and hadn't noticed that he had woken. They were holding Ethera, Edgar's sword and looking closely at the markings along the blade.

'Be careful with that,' murmured Edgar from the floor.

'Sorry,' said Joe guiltily before placing it carefully back on the floor next to Edgar. The Knight walked over to the mattress that Max was still sleeping in and pulled the blanket back so that he could look at his ankle. Not wishing to wake him he gently examined it; a lot of the redness had dissappeared and there didn't appear to be any permanent damage.

'Did you stay up last night trying to solve Hadwyn's riddle?' asked Scarlet looking at the spread of leaflets on the floor and the pool of wax from the burnt out candle.

'Yes, but I didn't get far,' he replied rubbing his eyes. 'All I worked out was that the Silver Bough is probably in Edinburgh. The hills above Edinburgh are often called Arthur's Seat or Àrd-na-Said as they say in Scotland, which also means Height of Arrows. But I don't understand the bit about Stevensons treasure.'

'What about this third line, *Amongst the thistles and under the crown*,' asked Joe who was reading over Hadwyn's riddle. 'The crown could refer to royalty. Does Scotland have a royal family?'

'Not any more. The Queen is the head of royalty for all of the British Isles, including Scotland,' explained Scarlet.

'I found a leaflet about Holyroodhouse Palace,' said Edgar as he started shuffling the papers in front of him trying to find the right one. 'The Queen stays at the palace when she visits. It's at the opposite end of the Royal Mile to the castle. Maybe our next clue is there?'

Joe had now picked up some leaflets and was starting to read them.

'Listen to this,' Joe interrupted as he read from the leaflet in his hands. 'The High Kirk of Edinburgh with its famous crown spire stands on the Royal

Mile between Edinburgh Castle and Holyroodhouse Palace. It contains the Chapel of the Order of the Thistle; Scotland's company of knights.'

At this point they all turned round to see Max sitting up on his mattress rubbing his ankle.

'I feel so tired,' he said dreamily. 'What's the Order of the Thistle?'

'As far as I know,' replied Edgar, 'the order is made up of the English Queen and sixteen Scottish Knights and Ladies. They are represented by the Thistle, the national flower of Scotland.'

'So it's a bit like King Arthur and his Knights?'

'In a way,' nodded Edgar.

'So the crown could refer to the spire above the chapel of the Order of the Thistle,' Scarlet said excitedly, 'it fits. Where's the High Kirk of Edinburgh?' she asked Joe who turned the leaflet over and read the title printed on the front cover.

'St Giles' Cathedral. It looks like its near to the train station we came in to yesterday.'

'Come on,' said Edgar with renewed energy, throwing Max his coat to cover him once again. 'Lets get some breakfast then we're off to the Cathedral.'

'Can I get some trousers first,' pleaded Max.

20. THE PATHOLOGY REPORT

Steven and Georgia sat together at a wooden table inside The Fox and Hound tucking into bacon and eggs.

Yesterday, after discovering that the box of meteorites was missing, Steven had driven them back to the pub. Georgia was still feeling shaken and had said that she hadn't wanted to be left on her own, so she stayed in Steven's room. As soon as her head hit the pillow she had gone straight to sleep leaving Steven sitting quietly at his desk writing down some notes about his first day in Parsley Bottom. He then accessed the secure MI6 internet site via the many coded log in pages and drafted an email to Sir Adam. He mentioned Mr McRae's box of Meteorites that had been stolen, concluding that there was no reason to suspect anything more than an opportunistic car thief. He also wrote about the other meteorites that they had found in the woodland which were now safely stored inside his room as well as including Doctor Carter's concerns over the apparent appearance of acid burns on the flesh of the arm in the river. He concluded by highlighting the similarities between what he had heard from Doctor Carter to what had been said in the meeting about the flesh eating bacteria. Steven suggested that Sir Adam contact Harrogate Mortuary to get the Pathology report done as soon as possible. He then clicked send and decided to catch up on some sleep, so made up a bed on the settee with some extra pillows and sheets he found in the wardrobe.

This morning his back was stiff and achy after spending seven hours lying down with his feet propped up on the arm of the settee, but eating the breakfast was starting to make him feel better, especially as it was washed down with strong black coffee. Georgia also seemed to be feeling better and was already eating her second helping of bacon which she had placed inside a soft bread roll together with a splash of tomato sauce.

'Morning Sergeant Allen,' said the landlord who doubled up as a waiter this morning. He was talking to the tall and now familiar figure of the Police Officer as he walked into the pub with a brown cardboard folder tucked beneath his arm.

'Coffee please Graham,' he replied as he pulled a chair up to Steven's table. 'Do you mind if I join you,' he politely asked Georgia, who shook her head.

'Mr Knight, you obviously know some very well connected people. I had a phone call from Doctor Carter last night; unknowingly he had been assigned two other pathologists to assist him with the examination. By all accounts they had been sent from London, colleagues of yours I would presume.'

He paused, waiting for Steven to respond, but as he didn't know anything about what Sir Adam had organised he continued to eat his breakfast.

Sergeant Allen held out the folder for Steven to take. 'Obviously it's not complete yet. We are still searching the river but this report will give you a lot more information about the arm we found yesterday. We've also identified who it belongs to, Bob King, an unmarried security guard who does the night shift at the Paper factory further up river from where the arm was found. He failed to arrive for work last night and there are signs of a struggle next to the river edge at the back of the factory.'

Georgia was quiet again, but at least this time she wasn't shaking.

Steven opened the report and started to skim through it to the area he was interested in while Sergeant Allen sipped his coffee.

> "Outer skin swabbed, paying particular attention to the areas underneath the folds of the skin on the palm of the hand which appear to hold an as yet unidentified substance. Clothing fabric was removed and taken for further analysis. Sections of the skin appear to have been melted away, more where the fabric from the shirt sleeve had not been protecting it. The edge of each hole was raised and uneven. No obvious sign of bites or teeth marks. General pH tests indicate an overly acidic nature to each wound. Overall skin colour is pale with patches of brown discolouration. Skin slightly swollen. Inside each wound the layers of skin had been dissolved away to expose the muscles beneath, some of which, from the pitted appearance, have also begun to dissolve. Wounds all at varying depths. Muscles are in a state of early decomposition which appears to be too quick for the approximate length of time the arm had been in the water. Apart from water, the wounds ooze a smelly, yellow liquid. Bone exposed on two knuckles, also degrading."

'How long before the results of the samples come back?' asked Steven who was wondering if Mr King's body had become infected by the alien bacteria whilst in the water, or more worryingly before it even entered the water.

'It could be a week if we're lucky. It depends on what they're looking for. Maybe you should ask your colleagues, all samples that had been collected, together with the arm itself, have been commandeered by MI6 and taken away.'

'Have you found the rest of Mr King's body?'

'Not yet. We did find his wristwatch in the river near the factory and several torn bits of clothing have turned up at various places further downstream. We were able to identify them from the name badge attached to one of them.'

As Steven and Sergeant Allen were talking, Georgia noticed that the landlord was pointing in their direction, he seemed to be telling a man that stood next to him who they were. The man was elderly and short with a balding head and he wore an old knitted jumper with threads and holes in various places. He walked towards the table and stood slightly away from them, almost not wanting to be impolite and disturb their conversation.

Steven became aware of the man standing there, as did Sergeant Allen who stopped talking and turned in his direction.

'Morning everyone,' he said to the three of them,' sorry to interrupt your breakfast,' he apologised to Georgia in his gentle Scottish accent as she bit into her bacon roll.

Steven stood politely as he recognised who the man was.

'Mr McRae, how nice to see you again,' he said.

'Mr Knight, glad you are still here. I don't know if I'm doing right by coming to you or not, but I thought you may want to see something else that I found.'

'More meteorites?' asked Steven excitedly, thinking that he could replace the ones that had been stolen, before looked nervously at Sergeant Allen, knowing that he had given away some information about the investigation he was undertaking, but his full attention seemed to be on Mr McRae and the black bin liner that was hanging by his side. From the way it hung, it was obviously heavy.

'No. Not meteorites, something else. It might be better if we go outside so that I can show you.'

Curiosity got the better of them all as they filed out behind Mr McRae and stood on the grass in front of the pub. He placed the black sack on the ground and picked at the knot. They all crowded around the bag silently waiting for the knot to untangle and the contents to be revealed. Once the bag was untied, he pulled the side of the bag up and something slid out onto the grass.

There was an over powering smell of decay and compost from what appeared to be a pile of cut grass and brown leaves in front of them. But there was more to it than just a loose pile of garden cuttings, whatever Mr McRae was showing them was solid and had form and shape beneath.

'What is it?' asked Sergeant Allen disappointedly.

'I was turning my compost last night and I found that,' he pointed at the mess on the grass. 'I didn't know it was there until it was too late and I saw one of the prongs on my garden fork sticking through it. It's some sort of animal I think.'

Steven knelt down and was now taking a good look at Mr McRae's deposit. 'Have we got any gloves in the field kit?' he asked Georgia who nodded and walked across the grass to the car, opened the boot and took a pair of latex examination gloves from the fabric bag she had been using in the woodland yesterday.

Steven slipped them onto his hands and started to remove grass and leaves from whatever was in front of him. It felt firm and cold under his hand and he was slowly revealing what looked like a blackened skin. He started to smooth some of the skin out and untangle the mass. As he lifted one of the blackened flaps of skin Steven suddenly jumped backwards with a sharp intake of breath.

'What is it?' asked Georgia who couldn't see what Steven was looking at.

'It,' he stuttered. His breathing was shaky, 'It… it looks like an eye.'

'What do you mean?' said Sergeant Allen as he too crouched down next to Steven.

'It looks like whatever this is has an eye,' Steven replied, 'and only one.'

He reached forward once again and lifted the flap of skin to reveal a single round milky white eye which was about the size of a golf ball with no central pupil.

Georgia cupped her hand to her mouth as she let out a small gasp.

21. ST GILES' CATHEDRAL

After they packed up their belongings, Edgar and the children left their attic room and made their way back into the centre of Edinburgh and down the Royal Mile until they came to the front of St Giles' Cathedral. Although the rain had stopped there was darkness in the sky that continued to cast a depressing blanket over everything. They approached the Cathedral from the direction of the Castle and could see the crown spire standing proud above the Cathedral building that was mentioned in the leaflet Max had read that morning. They passed a tall green stained metallic statue and walked up the stone steps to the west entrance. There were two ornate doors, one to let visitors in, the other to let them out, both were dwarfed by the grand archway decorated with numerous stone carved Gargoyles projecting their heads out from the ledge above the entrance ready to drain water from where it collected in the dips in the roof.

Edgar paid their entrance fees and they entered the Cathedral in single file. Max appeared to be more nervous than usual after his close encounter with the Moon Stealer the previous night. As they walked into the enormous space of the Cathedral they were immediately dwarfed by the stone columns that stretched high towards the ceiling before dividing into complicated finger like arches that reaching over to touch other pillars. Long thin colourful fabric banners hung down from each column, golden winged angels were embroidered into the fabric and seemed to trumpet their arrival. Whilst above them smaller flags stitched with crosses and crowns, horse heads and stars hung lifelessly from the roof. At the far end was a large blue stained glass window that towered higher over them as they made their way further into the Cathedral. They had not agreed on a plan about what they were going to do once they had arrived at the Cathedral, but they all seemed to naturally move towards the stained glass window, with their heads all looking upwards not knowing what their feet were treading on.

'What are we looking for?' whispered Max to Edgar, scared to break the peacefulness inside the Cathedral, but desperate to ask the obvious question.

'I'm not sure. Maybe we should start in the Thistle Chapel as it's mentioned in the riddle,' replied Edgar who had noticed a sign pointing them in the direction of a small chamber.

Edgar strolled off to his right and the children automatically followed. Through another stone archway they entered a much smaller room. Along both sides were wooden seats, carved animals making up the arm rests with highly detailed canopies that looked like crowns stretching upwards above each seat. On the backrest was the coat of arms of the Knight that the seat belonged to, like a name badge. On the ceiling the stone work was so fine that it almost appeared to be made from a fragile veil of lace that hung from the walls. The grey stone detail seemed to be alive with thistles in bloom and gold painted angels holding shields.

Once again, all they could do was look in amazement at the carvings of animals and the ornate paintings on some of the wooden panels. Edgar went over to the first chair and started looking at each coat of arms. Some had more shields on than others, but there were none that he recognised. Thick wooden carvings projected from the sides of the room and towered above where the Knight's heads would have been. On top of each of these was a carved painted animal. At the far end was a separate seat on which was the British Royal coat of arms.

'This must be where the King or Queen of England would sit,' Joe indicated to the large chair at the far end which was more prominent than any of the others.

'Do you see anything to do with Hadwyn in here?' asked Max.

'No. I don't even recognise any of the coats of arms that are on the chairs,' Edgar replied with a sad shake of his head.

Scarlet had been silent up till now. She had been thinking hard about the meaning of the words in the riddle. 'The Thistle is only referred to in the third line of the riddle,' she said, 'What about the second line, *And Stevenson's treasure is hidden from sight*, maybe that's the clue that we should be looking for?'

'But who is Stevenson?' asked Joe.

'I've been thinking about that and I have an idea. At school last year we had to do a project for English Literature about a famous author. My dad used to read Treasure Island to me when I was younger, so I chose its author for my project. His name was Robert Louis Stevenson and he's a Scotsman. What if the line in the riddle refers to Treasure Island, so Stevenson's treasure would be a book?'

'But Sir Hadwyn was a medieval knight, so wouldn't have known about Robert Louis Stevenson,' said Max.

'Edgar said he only died last year. If he wrote the riddle more recently, he would know about Stevenson.'

'But the third line said *Amongst the thistles and under the crown*. In this room we are *amongst the thistles* and we know we are *under the crown* as the spire on top of this Cathedral is known as the crown spire, so shouldn't it be in this room?'

'Maybe, but there's also another way of looking at it. Did you see the banners and flags in the main area of the Cathedral?' continued Scarlet.

'Yes,' replied Joe.

'Well they all have coats of arms on just like these seats so they must also represent the 16 knights of the Order of the Thistle. *Amongst the Thistles* could simply mean anywhere inside the Cathedral, not just in the Thistle Chapel.'

'So we're now looking for a book anywhere inside the Cathedral, probably by Robert Louis Stevenson?' Max said starting to feel like the task had become even harder than it had originally seemed.

'It makes sense Max,' said Edgar reassuring him. 'What have we got to lose?'

They all followed Edgar out of the Chapel and back into the main section of the building.

'Let's split up and look in different sections of the building.' Edgar coordinated everyone into different Aisles and Chapels within every corner of the Cathedral.

Joe went off towards the north side of the Cathedral to a section called Chambers Aisle. In front of him was a wooden panel between two columns of stone. Beyond it was a black and white tiled floor, a wall panel and two more stained glass windows. Joe couldn't see any books in this small separate section and there were no obvious connections to King Arthur or any Knights. He casually walked out; hands in his pockets feeling quite disappointed, but then happened to glance to the side where the Cathedral shop was. He walked up to a display stand of postcards and picked one of them out, paid for it then went back to the centre of the Cathedral to meet back up with the others.

Edgar had been walking up and down the centre of the Cathedral from the entrance to the large stained glass window at the east end examining every pillar and stone sculpture there was. Joe stopped him.

'I've found this,' he said showing Edgar the postcard he had found. Edgar looked at the picture on the front of the card then turned it over and read the description of the image on the back. By now Scarlet and Max had also made their way back to join the other two.

'Robert Louis Stevenson Memorial Panel, St Giles Cathedral Edinburgh,' read Edgar from the postcard, 'Scottish novelist and poet best known for works including Treasure Island, Kidnapped and Strange Case of Dr Jekyll and Mr Hyde.' He paused, 'Scarlet, you are a genius,' he said with a smile on his face.

'This must be what we're looking for!' said Scarlet in a restrained, but excited voice.

Edgar took the postcard over to one of the cathedral guides who was sitting at the entrance. The children could see the man pointing over to an area to their left. Edgar came back over to them.

'Apparently there's a large bronze panel on the wall close to the ground,' he said as he walked over to the south side of the building. 'Look down there. *The trusted and pure with head bowed down.* Bowing your head not only refers to the religious meaning inside the Cathedral, but he also wanted us to make sure we were looking down rather than up, as we have been doing ever since we came in here.'

They all stood staring down at the panel. The large brown waxy bronze plaque showed Stevenson sitting on a couch with a large blanket draped over his legs. In one hand was a pen, obviously ready to write, whilst the other supported sheets of paper upon his knee.

Scarlet knelt down on the cold stone floor and looked closely at the panel.

'There looks like there are some small words engraved on the edge of the paper,' she said. 'It looks like it says Pan's Pipes.'

'What are Pan's Pipes?' asked Max.

'I recognise the title,' said Scarlet thinking back to her project, 'I think it was a poem he wrote.'

'Didn't the second paragraph of Hadwyn's riddle mention a piper,' said Joe.

'You're right,' said Edgar as he thought about the riddle. *'Below the bridge, a piper alone.* It seems like we are on the right path, but where do we go from here?'

22. EDGAR TELLS THE TRUTH

They left the Cathedral under a damp fog which clung to their clothes making them cold and heavy. None of them had worked out where they were going to next on Hadwyn's trail so they decided to take a break inside a small coffee shop. They picked a table in the window and watched people walking past, their heads bowed down against the weather. Although they felt confident that they had unravelled some of the riddle, it didn't seem to point them in any clear direction. Edgar seemed to be deep in thought, he hadn't said much since they had discovered the panel inside the Cathedral.

'Why did Hadwyn leave a riddle anyway,' asked Max.

'To protect the Silver Bough of course,' replied Edgar, 'he couldn't just leave it somewhere obvious, otherwise anyone could find it and if they knew its true power they could open up many gateways between the Worlds of Men and Faeries without any sort of protection. This world has lost all sense of magic and would be powerless to stop the Faerie Queen from causing chaos and ruling both worlds.'

Edgar placed his notebook on the table and they all re-read the second part of the riddle:

> Below the bridge, a piper alone,
> The bard's sweet song turns water to stone.
> From one true touch the stone will part,
> And only be used by the brave at heart.

'What I don't understand is this Pan's Pipes clue?' said Max who's ankle seemed to be feeling a lot better. 'Are we looking for a musical pipe or the Silver Bough?'

'We found Stevenson's panel which mentioned the poem that he had also written, so maybe we need to be looking for that book next,' Scarlet said trying to keep their conversation positive.

'So why don't we get a copy of Pan's Pipes then and see what it says?'

'It's not that straight forward. Pan's Pipes is a poem and they are often published within a collection of other poems and I don't know what that book is called.'

'We could always find a book shop and ask, they may know which book it is included in,' interrupted Joe.

There was a small gap in the conversation whilst they all took a sip of their coffee.

'Do you think we should get home and warn everyone about the Moon Stealers?' said Max. 'If the creature we met in the tunnel under the castle has some brothers and sisters in Parsley Bottom, our families could be in danger.'

Edgar looked up from his cup, 'we are all in danger from them.' He seemed to look uncomfortable, 'I haven't been totally honest with you all.' He paused while the children stared at him waiting for him to continue.

'We do need the Silver Bough to enter the unseen world to find Peter. But we also need it for another reason. Back in my time, a mighty and powerful Astronomer called Putarin made a prophecy about the future. King Arthur trusted Putarin as he had demonstrated his skills on many occasions in advising Arthur on when the crops needed gathering before devastating floods or dry seasons ruined them. There was another time when a Knight from a neighbouring Kingdom called Sir Maughter de'Glise approached Camelot with a message from his King asking for friendship in exchange for the hand of one of the Princesses of the court. Arthur always wanted to bring peace to England so he took Sir Glise's offer and a lavish wedding was arranged. The whole of Camelot prepared for the wedding, gloriously coloured banners hung from all of the buildings, food was ordered from every corner of the Kingdom and dancers and singers where recruited to perform at the ceremony. However, the night before the wedding Putarin had studied the stars to see if the marriage was to be a successful one, but instead saw something much more important. He went to Arthur immediately and told him that King Seanal intended to poison Arthur and his Knights so that they could take over Camelot. On the day of the wedding King Seanal arrived at Camelot to a fanfare of trumpets accompanied by twelve of his bravest and most splendid Knights riding on horseback. He also brought with him a gift for Arthur of six wooden crates filled with many rare bottles of wines from his travels overseas. Arthur and his Knights kept a wary eye on their guests while his servants swapped the wine for bottles of Camelot's own. After the ceremony and in the Great Hall the feasting and celebrations began. Unknown to them King Seanal and his Knights were served the wine that they had brought with them whilst Arthur was not. The poison in the wine only took a few minutes to work and Camelot was spared an invasion. King Seanal's army waited around the outside of Camelot's walls for the signal to attack from their King that never came. Putarin had saved Arthur's life and Camelot's future. His words and prophecies were forever trusted and treated as law.'

The children had been quiet listening to Edgar's story.

'But what's that got to do with the Silver Bough?' asked Joe.

'The prophecy that Putarin made concerns the future of England and the joining of the Realms of Men and the Faerie World. Although Arthur found it hard to believe that these two worlds could ever come together again, the Prophecy was kept safely recorded due to the high regard Arthur held him in. The prophecy said that the two worlds may only come back together when England was in its greatest need. I believe that that time is now and using the Silver Bough is the only way to bring the worlds together.'

'But why is England in such great need?' asked Scarlet.

'The slime inside the church at Parsley Bottom could be similar to what we saw coming from that creature in the tunnel beneath the castle. If that's the case then we know there are more creatures out there and they could pose a huge threat not only to England, but to the whole planet. Two months ago there was a small meteor storm in the sky above Parsley Bottom. It doesn't take a scientist to be able to link the two things. It's possible that the meteorites have something to do with these strange creatures appearing across the country.'

'I remember hearing about that on the radio,' said Scarlet.

'So you think we have aliens running around Parsley Bottom?' said Max. The more he thought about the Moon Stealer that had grabbed him last night, the more he realised that it could be true.

'I'm afraid so Max. You see it's not only important that we find the Silver Bough so that we can rescue Peter, who's life is just as important as yours, but we also need it to save the Earth from a darkness that is probably already infecting England.'

'What exactly is the Silver Bough?' Scarlet asked Edgar.

'The Silver Bough is a magical item that was created many years ago by a Druid called Arawyn Claremont. He cut a branch from an Elm tree that stood in his garden and carved it into a curved flute shape with several slits for wind to be blown through and a series of finger holes to change the note. Arawyn performed strong magic upon it that he had learnt from the Ancients. To most people the bough would look like nothing more than a plain and dull wooden flute, but when held by the right hands it would turn to silver and play the most magical music. The music would enchant and possess certain animals as well as provide Arawyn his entrance into the Faerie World.'

'So are we looking for a wooden flute or a silver one?' Scarlet asked.

'It's not likely to be silver. It only changes to silver when it is held by the right person. It chooses its master, usually someone with some inherent magic. It may not even be made of wood. If you think back to Hadwyn's riddle, there is mention of stone in two of the lines; *"The bard's sweet song turns water to stone, from one true touch the stone will part."* I think it may be in the form of stone, to keep it hidden and protected.'

Edgar looked down at the brown swirls of coffee that had mixed with the white creamy top in his cup as if trying to read into the future. 'I'm not going to lie to you, the journey ahead will be dangerous,' he began, 'but I believe that this is the right path for me to take, if only to help Peter. I will continue on that path with or without you all. With your help I know we can find the Silver Bough, but after that I will ask nothing more from you. I will take you back to Parsley Bottom and you can finish your spring break and return to school as normal, if that is what you wish. I will continue through into the Faerie World to find Peter, alone if necessary.'

There was an uncomfortable silence.

'Are you kidding?' said Joe. 'There's no way I'm going to sit at home waiting to go back to school when I could help you find Peter. And if the Moon Stealers are as big a threat as you think, I want to do my bit to stop them. Certainly beats fraction and spelling homework.'

'Thank you Joe,' said Edgar as he looked up over his coffee cup towards Joe with a mixture of sadness and pride in his eyes, 'I know that you have an important part to play in this journey too.'

'Well you don't think I'm going to miss out on all of the fun do you?' said Scarlet with a smile.

The three of them turned to Max waiting for him to say something.

'I'm scared,' he said simply, 'but I think you need me.' He smiled at Edgar.

After they finished their coffees they walked along the shop fronts looking for a book shop to continue their quest to decipher Hadwyn's riddle and find a copy of Pan's Pipes.

23. BACTERIA ON THE MOVE

Against the wishes of Sergeant Allen, Steven had taken the decision to send the unknown thing that Mr McRae had delivered to the pub that morning down to London. The policeman had argued that it should be taken back to the police station for testing as it could be relevant to the investigation into the night watchman's death or Peter Crisp's disappearance. Once again, Steven's MI6 authority had over-ridden the policeman and Georgia had taken the animal to London herself, together with the water samples. Hopefully Coldred and his technicians would be able to give them some idea of what it actually was.

For the rest of the day Steven had decided to return to the woodland and try to follow the map that Georgia had marked on the day before. As he scanned the woodland looking for more meteorites he had peace and quiet to think. No walkers were allowed in the area because of the police restrictions around the crime scene, so he had the place all to himself. Even the birds seemed to have left the area; it was like he was walking around in an airless vacuum; all he could hear was the sharp intake of his own breath filling his lungs with oxygen.

In his head he was trying to make some sense out of what he knew so far, breaking the facts up into simple chunks of information. He now knew that the meteorite he had seen inside MI6 was not the only one to fall to Earth during the meteor shower and there was every possibility that some of the others also contained the same alien bacteria if they came from the same shower. In Steven's mind he knew it was likely that the alien bacteria was in the muscles of the dead night watchman and was probably responsible for killing him. Then this unidentified creature arrives. It had to be linked to the alien bacteria. The thought of a living alien scared him whilst at the same time made him feel excited. He had been working in MI6 for two years now and not found a trace of anything that could be classed as vaguely like an unexplainable foreign object. This though, was more than he could ever have hoped to find in his lifetime, an alien creature that could survive on Earth.

The metal detector gave off a loud high pitched squeal as it passed over something metallic. Getting his spade he didn't have to dig very far before he hit a discarded and rusty crushed drinks can. As he leant on the handle of the spade he looked down towards the riverbank where yesterday he had been sitting with Georgia.

Everything was centred around the river. As the previous samples of the water showed traces of the bacteria, it must be the river that was spreading the bacteria to other locations. The infection had already found its way inside a cow from Richard Baxley's land which was just beyond the woodland he was currently standing in. Thinking logically, the bacteria could easily have transferred some distance along the river as it divided into streams or joined up to other rivers. There was no way of knowing where the bacteria could end up. Wherever the water went, so could the bacteria as long as it could survive in the water. He remembered what Coldred had said inside MI6 that the bacteria only seemed to survive in damp conditions, but he also said it couldn't survive in sunlight, so would be confined to the darker areas of the rivers, such as underneath the muddy banks or in the darkness at the bottom of deeper water.

By lunchtime Steven had finished the area he was working on and decided to walk back to the pub stopping off at the local bookstore to buy an Atlas of Britain, as well as a limp ham and lettuce sandwich from the supermarket.

'Have there been any messages for me,' he asked the landlord as he picked up his room keys, but there hadn't been. Georgia had still not returned from London.

Steven's shoes echoed on the narrow staircase as he trod heavily on the faded red patterned carpet that covered the steps at the back of the pub, then he walked along the cream woodchip papered corridor to his room. He opened the door, propped the metal detector up against the wall in a corner and lay down heavily onto the bed. As his head sank into the soft pillow he caught the faint smell of Georgia's perfume that she had left on the pillow from the night before. He realised that he missed her company and hoped that he would hear her gentle knock on the door to his room soon.

He picked himself up from the bed and went over to the desk, taking a bite of the limp sandwich as he went.

He placed the atlas in front of him and opened it out so that he could clearly see the double pages that showed Parsley Bottom and its river. He traced it backwards into the higher land of the Yorkshire Dales where the river must naturally start as rain water collected before filtering down to lower ground. He then got a sheet of paper out of the desk drawer and started drawing the path of the river from Parsley Bottom, which was represented by a thin blue line and appeared to continue on through the small villages of

Newton Rise and Beckwith Green as well as others which didn't appear to be named. It then filtered into Thornback Reservoir followed by the larger Gouston and Swinesly Reservoirs from which the water drained into many other rivers and streams and on to Harrogate where it joined the Rivers Tidd and Ousse to York and Hull then into the North Sea.

Steven looked at the thickening blue line as it continued eastward towards the sea, branching into many other small rivers and streams destined for more small villages. Before it joined the North Sea, the River Humber divided off into the River Trent which penetrated deep into the heart of England. If alien bacteria landed in Parsley Bottom during the meteor shower it could already have reached densely populated areas like Nottingham and Birmingham. Maybe it had already spread further across England than he could possibly imagine.

Steven picked up the phone and dialled the number for Sergeant Allen's police station.

'It's Steven Knight,' he spoke into the mouthpiece, 'I need your help. I want to access the police database. I'm looking for any other reported deaths that might show similar marks to those we saw on the arm from the river. And I want to look in specific places including Nottingham and Birmingham. Yes, I know that will take time. Sergeant, remember that this is a matter of national security and you should not repeat anything you have seen or heard.' He hung up and leant back in the chair thinking once again.

If the bacteria was dangerous to humans, many thousands or even millions of people could be at risk if they came into contact with it and could all suffer a similar fate to that of the night watchman or the cow that had been sent to the abattoir.

The possibility of the bacteria being spread was huge. If the water systems of towns and cities near to airports became infected then it could already be being carried around the world on aeroplanes.

The other worrying form of transport was inside food. Coldred had mentioned that bacteria had already been discovered in a cow, but some may already have got into the food chain unnoticed. Steven stood up and threw the remains of his sandwich into the waste bin, walked over to his suitcase and pulled out his notepad. He flicked through the pages until he found the notes he had made on the train about the infected cow. It had been sent to Newton Rise Abattoir together with the rest of the herd by the farmer Richard Baxley two weeks earlier. The butcher who had noticed the strange colour in the meat was called Gilbert Rackham. Steven decided to make the most of his time and get the local bus to Newton Rise and talk to Mr Rackham as well as examine the paperwork so that he could trace the rest of the cows Mr Baxley had sent, but he was suddenly interrupted by a knock on his room door.

24. EDINBURGH CENTRAL LIBRARY

After visiting several modern bookshops Edgar and the children were still no further forward in obtaining a copy of Pan's Pipes.

Out of the corner of his eye, Max spotted a rusty sign hanging outside a shop front down one of the small old lanes leading away from the main pedestrian area. It sold antique books, and from the outside the building appeared to be as old as the contents it sold. They walked through an old fashioned door, the green paint pealing from the wood that framed each individual pane of glass. The shop itself smelt of dust and leather and very little light entered from outside. Floor to ceiling shelves were crammed with books in every available space, some shelves were so full that the wood bowed in the middle from the weight to rest on the top of the books directly beneath. There didn't appear to be many modern books in this shop, and those that were published more recently were piled in a corner, like they had been disapprovingly cast aside. It was quiet in the bookshop and none of the children dared to speak. It was like being in a very old library where everyone was reading and the slightest sound would disturb them and be frowned upon.

Edgar slid a book from one of the shelves that he was standing next to and began examining it closely. It almost looked like a piece of artwork. The orange brown leather spine had raised bands with gold lettering written on, while the front and back covers looked like thin slices of highly polished wood, the grain striped like the skin of a tiger.

'May I help you?' asked a small bearded man that looked suspiciously around a doorway. His face was pale but his beard was as black as ink. In front of his eyes he wore a thin pair of spectacles, balanced on his nose so that he could peer over the top of them. It was a miracle that the glasses stayed on his nose considering that the frame was twisted so much and taped together at the hinge.

'We're looking for a book,' said Edgar, who suddenly realised that it was a silly thing to start his question with considering they were inside a bookshop. He quickly continued, 'have you got a copy of Pan's Pipes?'

'Robert Louis Stevenson?' said the pale man as he looked thoughtfully at the ceiling. Joe withstood the urge to look upwards and see what he was looking at.

'I have several early copies of Stevenson's work on the shelf behind you, but I don't believe I have a copy of Pan's Pipes,' he replied.

'Do you know the name of the book that it is included in?'

'It was published amongst other papers in a book called Virginibus Puerisque. There are not many copies of it around but I'm sure there will be one at the Central Library, they have quite a collection of Stevenson books on display in one of the rooms under the bridge.'

Edgar took a sharp intake of breath. 'What do you mean by under the bridge?' he said, thinking back to the line in Hadwyn's riddle.

'You can find the library on George IV Bridge not far from the castle. There are four storeys of rooms built below the bridge, one of which houses a permanent exhibition to our countryman Robert Louis Stevenson.'

'Thank you so much, you have been a great help,' said Edgar with a large smile on his face.

Outside the shop Scarlet was the first to voice her excitement.

'The riddle must mean the bridge that the library is built on. *Below the bridge, a piper alone*. There must be something to do with Pan's Pipes inside the library that will actually take us nearer to finding the Silver Bough!'

They all felt excited once again to be back on the trail laid down by Sir Hadwyn and it showed in the speed they walked as they made their way back up the Royal Mile towards the castle. The dampness in the air no longer squeezed the energy out of them and they strode purposely past St Giles' Cathedral then turned left onto George IV Bridge. After a short walk they came upon an old elaborately decorated building that looked like it should have been built alongside a Chateau in France. They walked through the doors and were instantly surrounded by dark wooden polished shelves of books that had small walkways around the higher levels and cream and white stone pillars stretching all the way up to the ceiling. By contrast to the antique book shop they had just been in, the Library was organised and polished.

Joe had never seen so many books before and hadn't even known that so many actually existed. All of the books he had seen inside the mobile library that visited Parsley Bottom once a month could fit onto one shelf in this building.

'This way,' said Edgar in hushed tones as he noticed a sign directing them to the Stevenson Exhibition. They went through a door and wound their way down a black metal circular staircase until they reached the third floor. A darkened corridor with no windows was lit by a series of small lamps that hung on the wall and directed them beneath the bridge towards an exhibition space. There was a dark blue carpet here, not the highly polished wooden floor they had stood on in the entrance and it was worn slightly along the middle from the many feet that had walked along it. They all followed Edgar as he walked beside a wood panelled wall and into a room off the main corridor. It was a very plain room with nothing in it except a series of glass cases in the centre arranged in a square surrounding a stone plinth with a bronze statue on the top. The walls were hung with several small information plaques, as well as paintings and photographs of Stevenson at various stages through his life.

Looking into the glass cases were other visitors to the exhibition, as well as a library guide who patrolled slowly between the Stevenson Exhibition as well as the neighbouring Arthur Conan Doyle room.

Edgar and Scarlet moved around the cases looking closely at all of the contents until they came back to their starting point, whilst Max and Joe studied the pictures on the wall. The glass cases contained various books held open at certain pages, as well as other items that had belonged to Stevenson during his life.

'Have you found anything?' asked Joe as he looked over to Edgar.

'The book the man said contained the poem of Pan's Pipes is in this third cabinet, but the book isn't even open. Other than that there is no mention of Pan's Pipes. What about the pictures and photographs?'

'Nothing there either. They seem to chart his life and travels, rather than anything to do with his books.'

Edgar, Joe and Max stood staring into the cabinet, desperate to look inside the book to see what the Pan's Pipes poem said, but prevented by the thick protective glass. Scarlet went over to a small wooden bench that was pushed up against one of the walls and sat down feeling quite deflated that they had not found anything. Suddenly she sprang up and shouted, 'There!'

Everyone in the room turned and looked at the red haired girl who was now pointing directly at Edgar and the two boys. Embarrassed by her outburst she apologised to the other visitors and the guide who now stood watching her very carefully.

'Where?' whispered Joe, thinking that Scarlet must be seeing things.

'The statue in the middle,' she said as she walked over to them.

They all turned and looked at the statue in the centre of the arrangement of glass display cases. Standing on the top of the smooth cream stone pillar was a blackened bronze statue on a wooden base. Although the top half of the figure looked human, the legs appeared to be those of a goat. Held in his hands was a musical instrument made up of several tubes.

'That must be Pan.'

'Scarlet you are amazing, where would we be without you,' said Edgar.

'So is that the Silver Bough?' asked Max pointing to the musical instrument.

'No, I don't think so. The Silver Bough is one pipe,' replied Edgar. 'What the figure is holding is a collection of pipes of different lengths to make the different sounds. The hunt is not over yet, but we are getting closer.'

As they looked more closely at the statue they noticed that on the wooden base was a label that read:

Pan, God of the Wild
Presented to Edinburgh Central Library by the
Holyroodhouse Palace Arts Trust in commemoration of
the centenary of Stevenson's death
1994

'Holyroodhouse is the royal palace at the end of the Royal Mile,' recalled Joe. 'Looks like that's our next stop.'

25. A SHOCKING REVELATION

The knocking on Steven's door began again, this time slightly more urgently. He stood from the desk, cautiously opened the door and looked into the face of Georgia who gave him a kind, but nervous smile. Steven quickly realised that she was not alone as the tall figure of Coldred stepped out from the behind her and pushed open the door to enter the room. He was closely followed by Seward, both of them dressed in dark suits like they had just come back from a funeral.

Georgia lay a gentle hand on Steven's arm as she entered the room and sat herself on the edge of the bed.

Steven wouldn't expect the two men to come all the way from London to Parsley Bottom if it wasn't for a very important reason so he decided to be patient and wait and see what they said. By the time Steven closed the door Seward, who appeared to look quite a bit older than he had inside MI6, had already sat himself down at the desk and was looking at the sketch of the river map that Steven had drawn earlier in the day. Coldred was standing to the side of the window looking out to the green in front of the pub.

'What have you have found out so far,' demanded Seward who obviously didn't even have time to say hello and seemed to be in a very bad mood.

'Well, I spoke to Mr McRae, the gentleman who found the original meteorite and have since been carefully searching the land around his watermill for more meteorites. So far I have found a further two, all of which appear to be intact,' Steven decided it would probably be best not to mention the box of meteorites that had been stolen from the car to these two.

'Where are they?' interrupted Coldred.

Steven opened the wardrobe door, reached inside a bag and passed the two blackened meteorites to Seward.

'We took further water samples from the river and I also have a draft report from the Pathologist about the arm that we found,' he placed the piece of paper that Sergeant Allen had given to him that morning on the desk in front of Seward before continuing. 'The report describes the muscles and skin as being "in a state of early decomposition" which sounds similar to the description of the muscle changes in the cow that went to Newton Rise Abattoir, I'm sure you would agree that it would be a good idea for the Pathologist's samples from the arm to be tested for the alien bacteria. I've also mapped out the path of the river. If the bacteria is transporting itself through the water the extent of the contamination could become quite considerable.' Steven purposely hadn't talked about the strange creature Mr McRae had brought to them this morning, hoping that they would tell him what they had found out. There was silence in the room, Steven wondered which of them would talk first, finally it was Seward:

'We have some very dark times ahead of us Mr Knight, very dark indeed,' Steven wondered if the dark rings under Seward's eyes had anything to do with what he was about to hear. 'We are faced with a danger on a scale this planet has never seen before and unless we take action, we will never have the opportunity to see again. Our very existence as a race faces a much greater risk than we have ever encountered from any natural or manmade disaster in our entire history. How we act now will define the future of the human race as well as the world we live in for generations to come.' Seward's words hung in the air. Steven sat down next to Georgia on the edge of the bed. Suddenly the mood was very sombre.

They all looked at Seward, waiting for him to explain what he was talking about.

'The bacteria we found inside the meteorite is the same as that found in the river water as well as that found in the muscles of the cow. We heard yesterday that the man who worked at the Abattoir has also now died, as have his wife and a daughter. A third member of his family, the eldest daughter, is critically ill in an isolation booth in hospital. The Abattoir has now been locked down, all employees are being tested for the bacteria and so far 87% of them have tested positive and are now in a secure military wing at Selly Oak Hospital in Birmingham. I can also tell you that the arm you found in the river does indeed contain traces of the alien bacteria.'

'How are the workers from the Abattoir being treated if the bacteria is new to this planet?' asked Steven.

Everyone turned away from Seward towards Coldred as he spoke to them all, even though he continued to look out of the window. 'As the bacteria shows similarities to the Streptococcus bacteria or "flesh eating bacteria" that we already have on Earth, they are being treated in the same way with high doses of antibiotics as well as Hyperbaric Oxygen Therapy,' answered Coldred.

'What's Hyperbaric Oxygen Therapy?' asked Georgia.

'It's like a glass chamber that you lie down in. The Oxygen level is increased inside the chamber to control the infection and encourage healing.'

'Will they die?' asked Steven.

'Some will,' Coldred casually replied, 'some may not. We don't know yet. We are working on a vaccine that can make you immune to the bacteria, but until then we need you both to take a course of antibiotics just in case you've come into direct contact with the bacteria,' added Seward 'Some of the vaccines we have already tried have been successful in preventing the disease in the laboratory and all major UK drugs companies have now been ordered by The British Government to produce it as a matter of great priority.'

Steven was amazed at how much speed could be achieved when it was really necessary.

'Start taking these tonight,' instructed Coldred who threw a small box of tablets over to Steven and Georgia.

'But what about all the other people who may have come into contact with it. Some have had more contact than us; Mr McRae, Sergeant Allen, all the policemen who had contact with the arm in the river. Anyone could be carrying the bacteria, what about them?'

'The exposure of the alien bacteria to the wider public has become a greater risk than we first thought,' said Seward. 'Tomorrow morning a press release from the Ministry of Health will be reported on all news channels. In it there will be a statement about a new strain of Flu that has already caused illness across Britain and for the first time ever, everyone will be required by law to take the antibiotics until the vaccine can be found.'

'You mean you're going to lie!' shouted Georgia to the surprise of everyone. 'Shouldn't people know exactly what is happening? What about those people that decide not to go to the doctor and take the antibiotics?'

'They will probably die,' Coldred said without feeling.

'Miss Brown, we are faced with a very dangerous problem and need to act immediately so that we can save as many people as possible and protect the future of the human race,' said Seward gently. 'If the public knew the truth there would be mass panic, resulting in more death. We need to be able to provide an orderly programme of protection, it's the only way we can make sure that as many people are vaccinated against the bacteria as possible.'

'Believe me,' Coldred interrupted Seward, 'the bacteria is the least of mankind's worry. There is a much greater threat to come out of the meteorite than the bacteria; one we don't know how to protect ourselves from. Even if every one in the country was vaccinated we may still not be able to stop them from dying.'

Coldred moved away from the window and stood in the centre of the room almost like an actor moving across the stage to stand in his spot light. He paused for drama, making sure that all eyes were on him and he had everyone's attention before continuing his story.

'The thing that Miss Brown brought to London could be described as an animal,' he began, 'but certainly not one that exists on this planet. Do you remember what I told you about how quickly the bacteria was changing and how we constantly have to re-label it as the molecular structure changes?'

Steven nodded, thinking back to the meeting below MI6.

'After enough growing and feeding, that creature is a later version of the bacteria, but there's no way of knowing how it will change from here on.'

'But that's impossible isn't it?' added Steven in an amazed voice. 'How can something grow and change in such a short space of time,' he asked.

'This is something I've been thinking about too. Their fast growth could be caused by the difference in air pressure or gravity compared to that on their own planet. All planets have a gravitational force that sticks things to the ground, but on some planets that gravity is greater, making things heavier. If the gravitational pull on the alien bacteria's planet is different to our own, their growth rate could also be very different. For example, one of our years, could be equivalent to 100 of their years.'

Coldred pulled a thin portable computer from his case and pressed a button on the side. The screen flashed awake and after he pressed certain areas of the touch screen a series of pictures of small shapes dividing and growing began.

'This is a picture of a single particle of the alien bacteria inside a container. The time between each picture is only 37 minutes, but look how quickly the contents of the container changes. This picture,' he clicked onto another, 'was taken after just 11 hours. You can see from the cracks beginning to show in the sides of the plastic container that the volume of bacteria has increased so much that it is putting it under a huge amount of pressure.'

Steven and Georgia looked closely at the picture that was now on the screen. Inside the clear plastic container, a dark multicoloured mass similar to a fungus had grown and was now causing the plastic to crack and shatter like thin ice over a pond.

'When we received the animal this morning we took all precautions,' Coldred continued. 'Dissection of the creature was performed using the latest electronic laser cutting devices with robotic surgeons that were controlled from a separate room. Although the creature was at a far more advanced stage of growth than the bacteria we have grown in the laboratory, this shows all the signs that it was an infant creature.'

'You mean this was an alien child?'

'Yes. The creature was only two foot three inches tall and had no recognisable legs but it did have the shortened limb buds ready to develop into arms and legs. There was also the early development of a Patagium, similar to what bats need to fly.'

'What's a Patagium?' asked Georgia.

'It's the thin skin that stretches across the arm and fingers of a bat's wing. Without it they wouldn't be able to fly,' replied Coldred.

'So that alien creature we looked at this morning could actually fly?' Steven interrupted.

'Not yet. But presuming an adult developed in the same way, it would seem likely that this creature could fly. At the rate they grow it would only take around three days for the infant to become a fully grown, flying adult.'

'This is incredible,' said Georgia. On the screen of the computer, there were now some short films of sections of the creature being dissected.

'Unfortunately there is much more to this creature than first appears. It is actually a deadly chemical animal that is armed to kill. We found traces of several chemicals that could be excreted from under its skin. The first is a powerful Neurotoxic drug which would create a numb feeling in its victim, as well as muscle paralysis so that it became unable to escape or fight back. The second chemical is Nitric Acid and is used in a similar way to the acid inside your stomach, designed to dissolve and digest its food.'

There was silence in the room, Steven and Georgia couldn't believe what they were hearing, but they could see on the computer screen the creature they had unwrapped this morning on the grass outside the pub being examined by robotic probes.

'As well as having an impressive set of weapons, this creature is also developing some defences. Initially the bacteria in the laboratory showed signs of being sensitive to sunlight, but this variation has a thicker coating of cells on its back forming a hood-like cover over it's head area. These cells form an interlocking series of armoured tiles like those on a Woodlouse or Armadillo, still allowing flexible movement but with some protection.'

'How do they breathe?' asked Steven.

'They have a series of small openings around the body that lead into a network of air tubes similar to that of a Cockroach. They appear to filter Nitrogen from the air.'

'But if they don't breathe oxygen how can they survive? The air is made of Oxygen isn't it?' Georgia asked.

'You're right, there is oxygen in the air but only about 21%. 78% of the air is actually Nitrogen. Although we breathe Oxygen to survive not everything does, plants for example actually need the carbon dioxide from the air to survive. There are also 23 strains of bacteria on this planet that live in certain soil types that actually breathe Nitrogen; others use Methane from the atmosphere.'

Steven thought back to the morning when he had lifted some of that blackened skin up and seen what he thought was an eye.

'Can they see?' he asked.

'Yes but they only have one eye. The actual eye is not very good when you compare it with ours. We have a clear lens so that we can see effectively;

however, theirs is rather cloudy. This may protect their vision from the sunlight. They are able to adapt to their environment incredibly well. We have no way of knowing how these creatures will change, but we can only assume that they will change according to the conditions they are growing in.'

'This is unbelievable,' said Steven. 'It's like watching evolution at fast speed. Charles Darwin would be amazed.'

'What do these creatures eat to survive?' Georgia asked cautiously.

'Because of the rate of growth these creatures need a diet with plenty of protein in as well as other nutrients and the easiest way to consume large quantities of protein is by eating meat. Consuming animals such as cows and sheep will certainly supply them with proteins, but there's a bigger source of protein on this planet made up of 7 billion animals.'

'What animal's that?' Georgia asked.

'It's us. Humans.'

26. THE SILVER BOUGH

Once again Edgar and the children walked down the Royal Mile past the shops to the Queens Gallery and the entrance to Holyroodhouse Palace. Edgar had picked up some sandwiches as it was already late afternoon by the time they arrived. They quickly joined onto the last toured admission to the Palace and walked out into a large square courtyard together with the rest of the tour group. The guide began his well used speech about the history of the palace as well as providing some amusing facts, but neither Edgar nor the children were listening.

'*The bard's sweet song turns water to stone,*' Edgar repeated under his breath.

'What exactly is a bard anyway?' asked Joe.

'They were people who sang songs of Knight's courage and adventures,' whispered Scarlet.

'Maybe there's a statue of a bard inside the Palace.'

'I remember when we went on holiday to the peak district…' Max began before being interrupted.

'What's that got to do with the Silver Bough?' asked Joe as the tour group moved across the courtyard towards the entrance to the palace, above which the Royal coat of arms was carved into the stone.

'Well, I was thinking about the stalactites and stalagmites that grew inside the caves. They had been formed by water which turned into stone.'

'So you think we're looking for a cave beneath the Palace?'

'Possibly, but I was thinking more about that fountain over there,' replied Max pointing his finger in the direction of a tall algae covered statue that stood in the centre of the courtyard. 'This map says it's a Victorian fountain, although there doesn't look like there's any water coming out of it. But, if it's so old it may not be working anymore, so you could say that the water has turned it to stone.'

'It's worth taking a look,' said Edgar as he started striding towards the large ornate fountain in the centre of the courtyard. 'We'll catch up with you in a minute,' he shouted to the tour guide as the group continued towards the palace entrance. Edgar and the children now stood on the edge of a well groomed circle of grass looking up at the fountain.

Lion heads protruded from around the stone base whilst above it many different characters supported animals making up the arms of the crown shaped fountain at the top where statues of guards stood proudly holding their weapons. They all walked around the grass looking at the fountain from different angles for clues that might fit Hadwyn's riddle.

'Didn't you say that the Silver Bough was a simple pipe?' Joe asked Edgar.

'Yes. But it's not likely to appear in its silver form.'

'Well, there's a piper over here,' said Joe from one side of the fountain. They all crowded round to where Joe was standing and looked up at the figure he was pointing to. On one of the ornate supports that went up from the base, they looked at a stained green man with a round hat and a flowing cape who was frozen in time, blowing into a pipe.

'Does that look like the Silver Bough?' asked Joe.

'I can't remember in detail, it's so long since I saw Arthur presenting it to Hadwyn. It was a simple object with no jewels or gems, just a simple shaped flute with a series of finger holes.'

They all continued to look up at the statue and wondered if this really could be the Silver Bough that was in the hands of the stone piper. The back of the group of tourists had now gone through the main building doorway without them and apart from some tourists taking photographs of the palace, no one seemed to be paying the four of them and the fountain any attention.

'There looks like some writing on the base of the piper statue,' said Joe, squinting, 'it looks like the same style as the writing on the stones in the Faerie Ring, as well as on Hadwyn's shield.' They all squinted upwards trying to make out what was scratched around of the edge of the base beneath the piper's feet.

'It could just be the maker's mark,' suggested Scarlet.

'Or graffiti,' added Max.

Edgar strained his eyes to see the writing and took out his notebook, jotting down what was written.

The children waited while Edgar studied the letters.

A smile crept over his face. 'It's a message from Hadwyn,' he said excitedly, 'this is definitely the Silver Bough.'

'How can you be so certain?' Max asked.

'The writing is a series of letters, the first three are HSC, Hadwyn's initials; Hadwyn St Clair. Then a series of dots counting four and the last two are EG, my initials, Edgar Gorlois. It's a message: Hadwyn St Clair; for Edgar Gorlois.'

'Then we've found it!' Joe said.

Edgar nodded. 'All we have to do is take it from the statue.'

'*From one true touch the stone will part*,' muttered Scarlet as she recalled the next line of the riddle.

'What does one true touch mean?' Joe asked Edgar.

'Have you heard of the story of the sword in the stone?' Edgar replied. They all nodded. 'Well, this must be something similar, no matter how strong someone is or how hard they try, only one person can release the pipe from the stone bard. The true touch refers to the person who can remove the pipe, like King Arthur was the only one who could remove the sword Excalibur from the stone.'

The children nodded, remembering stories from their childhood as well as films that showed Arthur pulling Excalibur from the stone.

'Hadwyn's riddle said that the stone would part, but only for someone with a true touch so there's only one way to find out if this is the Silver Bough and that's to see if one of us can remove it from the piper's grip.' He paused as he looked around the courtyard, 'keep an eye out for an official,' he instructed to the children as he stepped over the grass and climbed onto the base of the fountain. He climbed up until he was standing next to the Piper. Worried that someone would see him, he quickly examined the piper then tried to remove the pipe, but it was secure and would not loosen from the piper's grasp. He jumped back down again and went to stand next to the children.

'It didn't work,' said Scarlet. 'You're Hadwyn's brother as well as a knight of King Arthur; surely it would recognise something familiar in you to that of your brother? Maybe this is all wrong, maybe this isn't the silver bough after all and we need to look inside the palace.'

'But maybe I'm just not the right person,' replied Edgar thoughtfully, 'Excalibur couldn't be pulled from the stone no matter how strong the knight was. An unlikely person in Arthur was the one it was waiting for. If this is the Silver Bough it will chose the right person. Each one of you now needs to try. It will recognise something in the sole of the person touching it and willingly give itself up.'

Scarlet stepped towards the fountain and Edgar lifted her up onto the base. She then climbed further until she was standing alongside the statue of the piper.

'Don't move!' instructed Edgar urgently to Scarlet as he noticed an official looking man walking across the courtyard towards them. As he approached they could see from the embroidering on his sweater that he was employed by the Palace. His walkie-talkie buzzed with interference.

'If you wish to get the full tour of the palace in before closing time, I would suggest that you shortly made you way inside,' he said to Edgar.

'Thank you,' replied Edgar, 'we will.'

The official glanced up at the fountain that he had seen every single day since he began working at the Palace.

As he was just about to turn and go, he hesitated, as if he had spotted something that was different to the other hundreds of times he had looked at the fountain. Edgar, Max and Joe held their breath, expecting the man to tell Scarlet off for climbing on the statue, but instead he reached up to the nearest lion's head and picked a hard, stale piece of chewing gum from its forehead. He tutted loudly then walked away towards the entrance of the palace. Edgar and the children couldn't believe that the man hadn't seen Scarlet, but as they looked up towards the statue, they couldn't see her either. Slowly, from behind the stone cape of the statue, Scarlet's red hair began to peer out. She smiled nervously and waited for Edgar to give her the all clear sign before she stepped out. Reaching up to the pipe she grasped a hand firmly around it and pulled slightly, trying to slide it from the piper's grasp.

Nothing happened.

Edgar lifted Scarlet down, checked once again that no one was watching them then helped Joe up to the statue. He too reached up and grasped the pipe with one hand and gave a gentle pull, but nothing happened.

After a couple of seconds a faint but high pitched mellow whistle erupted into the air, as if the stone piper was actually playing the pipe. Joe quickly withdrew his hand, but where his fingers had been it appeared as if he had left an imprint on the pipe like a shimmering coating. It reflected light like the mirrored surface of a pool of mercury and slowly the green algae discolouration changed into a shining silver pipe. Joe looked down at Edgar who gave him an encouraging smile. He reached up once again and this time the silver bough slid effortlessly from the piper's stone grasp and into the surprised hands of Joe. The sweet singing of angelic voices filled the air, making Joe feel like he was floating in a dream.

'You've done it!' said Scarlet in amazement, bringing Joe out of his dream like state, 'you're the one the Silver Bough has chosen.'

He jumped off the fountain and immediately the others crowded round him to get a good look at the Silver Bough. They were all surprised to see how plain it was. There were just a few simple carvings etched into the shimmering surface around the mouth piece and the exit.

'The Silver Bough chooses its owner,' explained Edgar to Joe, 'there must be many good reasons why it has chosen you.'

As they looked at the Silver Bough in Joe's hands, there seemed to be something magical drawing Max and Scarlet towards it. They felt an overwhelming urge to touch the surface, but before they got the chance, Edgar threw an old cloth over it. The distant sound of soft voices that sang in a language Joe did not recognise stopped suddenly as if the Silver Bough had been turned off at the touch of the cloth.

'We need to leave as quickly as we can,' said Edgar urgently, 'Joe, you need to hide the Bough where no one can see it.'

They left the courtyard of Holyroodhouse Palace and walked back towards Waverley Station, where they had arrived in Edinburgh only the day before. Inside the station the children stood together whilst Edgar went to get the tickets for the next train back to Harrogate.

'It will be nice to see our families again,' said Scarlet to the other two.

'Can I have another look at it?' asked Max curiously. 'I wonder if it would have released itself for me too.'

'I think I should probably keep it hidden,' said Joe as he nervously looked over to where Edgar was talking to the lady inside a ticket booth.

'It can't do any harm just showing me.'

Joe reluctantly lifted one side of the cloth from around the Silver Bough and almost immediately the angelic sounds started to fill the air like wisps of smoke circling around them. They received some odd looks from people as they walked past to get onboard a train, but everyone was too busy to stop and see what was producing the noise. Max looked longingly at the highly polished surface of the Silver Bough. His hand reached out towards it and his fingers lightly brushed the surface. Suddenly, the inside of the train station was filled with an ear piecing screech like an animal crying in pain. Joe nearly dropped the pipe as the scream pierced his ears, whilst other people in the station instinctively put their hands up to cover theirs. Max immediately removed his hand from the metal surface and took a step backwards. Although the sound had only lasted for a second, they could all hear it ringing inside their heads.

Joe was suddenly aware of an adult standing next to him, a look of fury on his face. 'Don't ever touch it again!' said Edgar in anger to Max as he threw the cloth back over the Silver Bough. 'Put it away!' he spat to Joe.

'What happened?' asked Joe nervously.

'Once the Silver Bough has chosen its owner, anyone else that attempts to use it will become tormented by the screams and curses of the lost souls that are trapped between the two worlds. Souls of those that are neither dead nor alive. Eventually they would drive you mad until you choose to take your own life and join them.'

They all sat in silence waiting for their time to come when they could board their train. It was now getting late and as the train pulled out of

Waverley station they could see that the greyness of the day had now turned into the darkness of the night.

The train rumbled along the track and soon all three children had dropped off to sleep. Edgar forced himself to stay awake, the train now carried an important cargo on its journey to Harrogate; a magical instrument that could only be used by its chosen owner. It was his duty now to protect and guide the children into a world they could not possibly imagine, but for now he let them sleep.

27. ATTACK ON PARSLEY BOTTOM

The hole beneath Parsley Bottom church began nearest to the river but extended into a maze of tunnels that went deep underneath the foundations of the church. Every now and then the tunnels opened out into large caverns that river water also seeped into, cascading down the walls into a muddy pool of water at the base. The caverns smelt of mould and metal. If anyone had actually tried to explore the tunnels they would find that the smell made their eyes water and their breathing difficult, as well as having pools of Nitric acid to avoid. There was a constant dripping sound from above, but not from rain water draining through the soil and rocks but from a yellow slimy liquid that dripped from the ceiling. On the ceiling black shadows hung upside down like bats in a cave holding on by their claw like toes gripped around the deep roots of trees.

The network of tunnels and caves were becoming overcrowded and the growing that the creatures had done so far had used up all of their energy reserves leaving them hungry and restless. A primal instinct instructed them to leave the nest in search of food tonight. The first dark shadow pulled itself through the hole; its body covered in a protective frothy slime and lay on the grass beneath a gravestone still and quiet. Then a sucking noise rattled from the breathing holes around its body as it pulled in air. A black leathery membrane slid up revealing a clouded eye that twitched rapidly as it took in the surroundings. It slowly pulled itself up into a kneeling position then unexpectedly thrust a skeleton like black hand out to pierce the soft belly of a rat that had cowered against a mossy stone tomb. The rat wriggle, trying to work itself free from the yellow hooked nail it was skewered on. The black creature lifted the rat closer to its eye, intrigued as well as amused by the little animal, but the hunter in it knew that this animal was a source of food. It pushed the rat into its circular mouth that was rimmed with small hook like teeth then let out a breathy screech that cut through the night air like a fingernail being pulled down a blackboard.

A second and then a third creature followed.

Before long the graveyard was covered with a small army of identical creatures, black and leathery and covered with a silver-like slime.

As some of the creatures began to experiment with walking and coordination, they began to lurch in the direction of some small cottages further upriver from the graveyard.

Others waited with their arms outstretched allowing the fragile skin that joined their arms to their body's time to dry, like a grotesque butterfly emerging from its chrysalis. Eventually they began beating their arms, slowly at first, feeling the resistance of the wind, but then faster until their bodies began to lift gently off the ground. Eventually they began to feel the strength in their arms and they flew towards the town.

As it was early evening there were still some people around Parsley Bottom, walking home from the pub or a meal out. Tom and his girlfriend, Emma were sitting on a wooden bench facing the park watching their friends play on the swings and slides; it was the only chance the teenagers got to play on them once all the little children had gone home. Tom laughed loudly as his friend nearly fell off the swing as it arced high into the air. Emma rested her head gently on Tom's shoulder and looked up into the night sky. The swings seemed to be making a lot more squeaking tonight than normal, or so she thought.

Suddenly Emma sat upright with a confused look on her face, squinting as she tried to examine the sky more closely.

'What is it?' asked Tom.

'Nothing. Probably just a bat,' replied Emma, who dismissed the shape she had seen in the sky.

Neither of them noticed the dark creatures that swept down from above to pluck them effortlessly off the bench. Tom managed to hold onto the arm of the bench as he was being dragged rapidly upwards into the sky, but its weight made him drop it to the ground. It was only then that his friends looked over to where Tom and Emma had been sitting and saw the bench overturned and empty. But they didn't have any time to wonder where their friends had gone as they quickly became the next victims of the night.

Slowly, the children's swings in the park squeaked backwards and forwards until they came to a stand still all on their own, the seats empty.

In another part of town two women stumbled out of a restaurant, arm in arm and laughing loudly. They began to walk down a narrow road that was enclosed on both sides by houses and only seemed wide enough for one car to drive down. Pippa had gone out that night to celebrate her birthday with a few friends, one of which, Beth, was now helping to take her home. The road widened and revealed a small square with parking down the centre. Beth reached inside a small handbag, took her car keys out and pressed the central locking button on the key fob. The orange hazard lights flashed and the doors unlocked. Beth opened her door ready to get in but then noticed that Pippa had fallen to the ground and was now sitting on the floor clutching her ankle.

'What are you doing there?' shouted Beth as she left the car and walked over to her friend.

'I've broken the heel of my shoe.' Pippa pointed over to a small grate at the side of the road for draining the water away. The narrow heel on her shoe was wedged in the gap between two of the metal bars. 'I think I might have twisted my ankle.'

All of their movements were being watched with some curiosity from above by creatures that until now were unfamiliar with humans, but they recognised an animal when it was vulnerable and they knew that she could not run and would make an easy target. Whilst Beth had gone to help her friend, several of the creatures had been curious about the car, some had gone underneath it whilst another had entered through Beth's open door.

'Come on,' encouraged Beth as she helped lift Pippa onto her good foot so that she could hop slowly towards the car.

Once the two girls had got themselves inside the car, the dark shadow struck, desperately consuming the source of meat. Up until now it had used a lot of energy to grow and evolve; now it needed to replace what it had used. The car shook from side to side; Beth and Pippa had no chance of escape from the unexpected attack.

All through the night the creatures feasted on any animal they came across; dogs, cats, cows, sheep and humans, they didn't mind which, it was just a source of food to them. Hundreds of creatures swamped Parsley Bottom during the night. People disappeared without a trace and homes with open windows were raided leaving nothing more than a slimy mess.

The assault on Parsley Bottom was just a small part of what happened across the rest of England on the same night. A new predator was lurking in the sky, fixed on an unchanging mission to feed their bodies and survive.

28. RUNNING INTO DANGER

After Coldred and Seward had left, Steven and Georgia ordered dinner from the bar in the pub and were now sitting on the bed going over what the two men from MI6 had told them. Georgia couldn't believe that it was actually possible for humans to be a source of protein for these alien creatures to feed on. More incredible was the simple fact that an alien bacteria had developed freely on the planet into a living creature and was surviving. She thought back to what Seward had said;

'Mankind has not had a predator since the age of dinosaurs. Until now.'

'We must act quickly,' Steven had said to the two men who didn't seem to feel the urgency that he did. 'People need to be warned.'

'As we already said, mass vaccination will be used to prevent infection from the bacteria. But, the unknown part is what to do once they reach the creature stage.'

'I already have some of my team working on the creature Miss Brown brought to us,' informed Coldred, 'we are trying to develop some form of equipment that emits ultra violet light, as well as chemical weapons but it's still early days.'

'We also don't know how the creature will change as it develops and grows. It could quickly adapt to any weapons that we might use on it, which would make them useless. At the moment we are resorting to conventional equipment such as guns and incendiary weapons. But the biggest challenge we face is that we don't know how many creatures actually exist. At the rate of growth we saw in the laboratory there could already be hundreds if not thousands in this area alone.'

'How can we find them?' Steven had asked.

'They don't appear to be warm blooded animals so they won't show up on any heat sensitive cameras. We have to physically look for them with our eyes, but we can't bring in the army to do it. We would have to evacuate the whole village and prevent anyone coming in or out whilst we search. Unfortunately this would create too much publicity and media attention. Once again we need to do things discretely to prevent panic and chaos.' Seward paused, 'your role in this has now changed, we want you and Miss Brown to start searching for the creatures. We will give you weapons and additional boxes of antibiotics.' He laid a black case onto the desk, flicked the metal clasps and showed them two hand guns embedded within a shaped foam interior, together with several additional ammunition clips and two boxes of antibiotics.

'But Sir, I wouldn't know where to start looking?' protested Steven.

'The arm that was found has been identified as being from a security guard that went missing from one of the factories up river, so start there. Locate the biggest concentrations of creatures and we can send in a small team of soldiers to exterminate them.'

'What does Sir Adam think?' asked Steven who suddenly noticed that his superior hadn't joined the other two men on their trip from London.

There was an uncomfortable silence in the room as the two men looked at each other.

'Sir Adam's body was pulled out of the Thames this morning. He drowned,' Seward explained. 'He was seen walking across Tower Bridge last night and an anonymous witness rang the Metropolitan Police saying they saw a man jump.'

Steven was stunned. He hadn't thought that Sir Adam was the sort of person who would have taken his own life. Especially now that alien life had been found on the planet, something he had been searching for his whole life and was as desperate to discover real evidence as much as Steven was. Something didn't seem quite right. He recalled his commanders warning about not trusting the other two men when they had walked to the secret meeting beneath MI6 and wondered if they had anything to do with his unexpected death.

As they sat on the bed picking at the food in front of them, neither of them feeling particularly hungry, their thoughts were interrupted by a frantic screaming from the front of the building. Steven jumped up and went over to the window but couldn't see anyone. As he scanned up and down the road he noticed dark shapes moving in the sky, diving at random intervals towards the ground.

'Georgia,' Steven said nervously, 'come and look.'

As she came to join Steven at the window, someone from the bar had walked out onto the green to see where the scream came from. As he stood looking around him he failed to notice a black skeletal creature swoop down and grasp his shoulders with the hooked claws that sank deep into his flesh. The man's scream was soon muffled by the black figure as it folded itself around the man's head to begin the process of digesting.

'It's one of the creatures,' Georgia stuttered in disbelief.

'We have to do something,' said Steven as he took a gun from the case that Seward had given him. The other gun, cartridges and antibiotics he stuffed into Georgia's bag and swung it over his shoulder.

'Come on,' he said, trying to encourage Georgia to move from the spot she seemed stuck to, 'apart from us no one else knows about the creatures and the danger we're all in. We have to help them.'

She had never felt as insecure as she had done in the last two days and was glad to have Steven to talk to, but what she had just seen terrified her so much that she wanted to close the curtains and try to forget what she was involved in. Steven pushed her coat into her hand and pulled her away from the window.

As they walked down to the bar area Steven had his gun ready in case one of the creatures had entered the building, but round every corner they found no creatures or humans. The bar was empty and the only thing they could hear was the gentle squeak of the metal sign hanging above the front door outside as it rocked in the breeze.

Georgia held tightly onto Steven's hand as they walked towards the door.

'Come on,' Steven said, breaking the silence. Georgia gave a little jump.

He pushed gently on the door until it opened just a little before daring to open it further. At first all he could see was the grass in front of the pub as well as Georgia's now familiar black car but there was so much about the scene that didn't look right. He could count at least two cars that had crashed into each other, one engine still smoking, the other completely crumpled. There were muddy tyre marks scarring the grass and some plants and flowers that had been uprooted were now spread across the road. For as far as he could see there was chaos and destruction.

He looked as much as he could up and down the road checking for creatures, as well as towards the top of the building, but there were none he could see except for some shadows in the distance darting erratically in the sky.

As Steven pushed the door open some more it hit against something.

Looking around the door he could see that one of the hanging baskets that had been fixed to the wall above the front of the building must have fallen down and was now preventing the door from fully opening. Steven cautiously squeezed himself through the opening and checked once again in all directions before stepping out of the pub. He then moved the basket from behind the door so that he could open it fully to allow Georgia to follow, staying as close to Steven as she could.

Walking onto the mounded grass in front of the pub gave him a good vantage point to look from. In every direction there seemed to be something out of place. Trees had been knocked down or were bent at peculiar angles. House windows were smashed. In the distance he could hear more screams and could see lights being turned on in house windows as curious people looked out to see where the noise was coming from.

Some spots of rain began to fall, but nothing would wash away the scene around them. A storm was brewing and the air felt electric and alive.

Steven ran over to the nearest car that had crashed or been left abandoned and looked through the smashed window. There was no one sitting behind the driver's wheel just a single shoe resting on the seat. He noticed a certain amount of sticky liquid that had dripped from the roof onto the ground. There were also two long scratches running down the length of the roof and above where the driver should have been the metal of the roof had been prized open like the lid from a can of beans.

'Look at this!' Steven shouted across to Georgia who seemed to have been glued to the pavement in front of the pub door. He had now leant closer to the car and was loosening something from between two pieces of metal around the roof.

He walked over to show Georgia.

'It must be a claw from one of the creatures. Coldred was right, the one that you took to London this morning was just a baby, they've developed into something a lot bigger and deadlier,' he said showing her what was in his hand. It was about as long as his little finger and curved and pointed. At the thicker end it was untidy and ragged like it had been pulled out of something.

'What if they come back?' Georgia asked as she continued to look around her for any more creatures.

'Look over there!' Steven pointed excitedly towards a figure he could see sitting inside one of the cars further up the road.

'Hello!' he shouted as he casually jogged down the road. As he got nearer to the car, he could hear the gentle hum of the engine running.

'Hello,' he tried again, 'are you alright?' The person sitting in the driver's seat didn't move. Her hands were gripped around the steering wheel. Now that he was nearer to the car Steven could see that although the person's eyes were staring straight ahead of her, she wasn't blinking. He walked around to the driver's side of the car and realised that the lady was probably dead from the look of her pale white skin and blue lips.

Steven tried the door handle, but it was locked. Looking around him he found a brick on the road that must have become loose from the impact of a car against a small stone wall and used it to break the window. He then reached in, unlocked the door from the inside, took the keys out of the ignition and placed his fingers on the lady's neck. He waited for several seconds but could not feel the faintest beat of a pulse.

'Is she dead?' asked Georgia reluctantly.

'Yes. Probably had a heart attack out of fear. Look how her hands are gripped around the steering wheel.'

Suddenly the night air was shattered by an explosion near to them. A jumble of black skin fell from the sky and landed on the roof of the car they were looking in making Georgia shriek with surprise. Steven instinctively looked up for other creatures before turning to where the explosion came from.

A man was now approaching them from within the wooded area on the other side of the road. He had a green waxed jacket on and some thick sturdy walking boots, but most menacingly of all, the smoking barrel of a shotgun was pointing in their direction.

'You shouldn't be out on the streets. Those things are everywhere,' as he said it he had walked to within a few feet of Steven and Georgia. 'You better get under cover and quickly, the sound of gunfire could make them curious. There are others coming this way.' He swung his shotgun up into the sky, using it to point at some more black shadows that were now flapping their way towards them.

A creature landed on the pavement beside the car, Georgia screamed and together all three of them backed away towards the other side of the road. More shot flew from the barrel of the man's gun exploding a hole in the body of the creature.

'Into the wood. The trees will give us cover.'

As the gun fire echoed across the sky, they turned and ran into the woodland and away from the creatures that now descended on the crashed car, feeding on the bodies of the two other creatures as well as the dead woman at the wheel.

29. BISHOPS GREEN STATION

Joe woke up suddenly. He was still tightly gripping the cloth that covered the Silver Bough. He found it hard to hold onto as he kept feeling the cloth sliding against the shiny surface of the pipe; it was almost like it wanted to get out from its cover. It took him a few moments to remember where it was that he had fallen asleep, but as his brain started to orientate itself, he realised that although he was inside a train carriage, the train was no longer moving. He looked over to the other children, they were all asleep but Edgar was no where to be seen. Looking out of the nearest window, all Joe could see was his own reflection, but on the other side of the carriage a couple of lights lit up a small station house. There were a few people walking along the platform talking to others and further up the platform, underneath a hanging clock he could see Edgar talking to the station master.

The engine of the train appeared to be completely turned off, no hum vibrated through the wheels of the carriage and the overhead lights appeared to be dim and probably running off a back up battery. Joe waited patiently enjoying the peace and quiet.

'Looks like we might be stuck here for a while,' whispered Edgar to Joe as he walked down the centre of the carriage towards him, 'there's some sort of communication problem.'

'What do you mean?'

'Well the driver can't get any response from Harrogate Station. We can't approach the station if they don't know we're coming, there could be chaos with the other trains or maybe an accident, so we have to sit here and wait whilst they keep trying.'

'How long have we got to wait?' said the sleepy voice of Scarlet who had opened her eyes at the sound of Edgar's voice.

'I don't know yet.'

Joe and Scarlet closed their eyes again and drifted into a light sleep while Edgar sat patiently waiting for something to happen. Ever since they had found the Silver Bough Edgar had felt a strange feeling growing. He was nervous about the journey ahead, not the one on the train, but going through into the unseen world to find Peter and he hadn't got any idea where to start looking. The children had put their faith in him during the search for the Silver Bough, but would they have so much confidence in him once they had gone into the other world.

Edgar was stirred from his thoughts by a series of thumps and bangs from a carriage further down the train which he took for nothing more than carriage doors slamming shut as passengers got back on the train. He looked out of the window towards the platform, in the reflection of the window a black shadow seemed to pass on the opposite side of the train as rapid as the blinking of an eye. Everyone that had been standing on the platform before had now disappeared; the platform was deserted. Edgar assumed that the train was getting prepared for departure once again so settled into his seat expecting to hear the ignition and hum of the engine as it fired into life ready to take them on the last leg of their journey. Instead he heard the screams of panic and more thumps and bangs from further down the train. Edgar stood and turned to look straight down the centre of the train through the glass of the interconnecting doors and straight into a scene of panic and destruction. Other passengers were climbing over the backs of chairs and tables, desperate to escape whatever was inside the carriage with them. Instinctively, Edgar woke the children, holding a finger to his mouth to tell them to be quiet, then grabbed the bag from the overhead rack and started pushing them in the opposite direction towards the nearest exit. He kept the children moving, preventing them from seeing what was happening further along the train. As they reached the exit, he turned around once again and looked down the train. One man was being pulled through a hole in the carriage roof by a pair of thin black arms, the claws deeply embedded in his chest. An elderly woman appeared to be held by a black creature similar to the one that the children had named a Moon Stealer from the tunnels under Edinburgh Castle. The creature had hold of the lady's head as if it was about to give it a kiss, but when it withdrew its hands, flesh seemed to peel away from her face as if it was made of jam. She fell to the ground behind the back of a chair and was instantly dived on by at least two more Moon Stealers.

At the exit door Edgar checked that it was safe for them to get off the train. There was still no one on the platform. Edgar withdrew Ethera, his white bladed sword and carefully stepped off the train. He signalled for the children to stay where they were whilst he quietly walked backwards towards the station building. As he got further away from the carriage he began to get a better view of the whole of the train. Further down the length of the train the roof appeared all twisted and torn and he could see the Moon Stealers flying in and out of it. Whilst keeping a careful eye on the other carriage Edgar signalled to the children to come over to him one by one. Joe stepped off first, followed by Max. At the back of the line Scarlet turned and looked further down the train and saw the creature's lifting bodies out of the train and taking them into the night. She started to let out a high pitched squeal before Edgar leapt at her and clasped a hand tightly around her mouth. The Moon Stealers didn't appear to have noticed. Edgar signalled to Scarlet that she must be quiet, but he could see the fear in her eyes. They both carefully and slowly stood up and joined Max and Joe who were already inside the Station building waiting room.

'It's the Moon Stealers,' whispered Joe to Edgar, 'like the one we saw in the tunnels under the castle.'

'We cannot waste any time. We must go through the gateway into the Faerie World, find Peter and as the prophecy said, unite the worlds to save England.'

'How far are we from Parsley Bottom?' asked Max.

'We've stopped at Bishops Green; it's about eight miles from Parsley Bottom,' Edgar glanced over to the carriage that the Moon Stealers were attacking. 'It looks like we've got off the train without being noticed and the Moon Stealers will have plenty to keep themselves occupied with here for some time.'

'But all those people,' said Scarlet desperately, 'can't we help them?'

Edgar sadly shook his head. 'No. The three of you and the Silver Bough are more important than an entire train full of people.' He turned away and started to look out of the windows on the other side of the station building, scanning the dark sky for any signs of any more dark creatures.

'Come on, let's get out of here,' said Edgar, satisfied that it was safe to leave the building. He slowly pulled the door inwards and slipped his head out so that he could have another look outside. At the back of the building there didn't appear to be anyone around, but he could see that there were three cars parked facing the front steps of the building, one of which seemed to have its door open. Edgar crept out of the building keeping his head low and hid within the gap between two of the cars. The children followed in the same manner, all the time watching the sky and checking behind them.

'Wait here,' Edgar whispered as he inched his way to the back of the car. If he raised his head high enough, he could see the Moon Stealers still attacking the train so he kept low, holding onto the bumper of the car as he moved around towards the one at the end of the row that had the open door. As he looked around the side of the car towards the door he could see the body of a man that lay half in and half out of the car, wedged beneath the open door. His shirt was in tatters showing deep red slashes across his chest. Patches of skin on his face and hands appeared to have dissolved and chunks of flesh had been gouged and torn from his body. Edgar crawled on the floor, hoping that the open door would shield him from the eye of the Moon Stealers. He pulled the body of the man out of the car and placed it on the floor then found the car keys within the man's blood soaked trouser pockets. Edgar slipped into the driver's seat and tried to close the door as quietly as possible but couldn't help making a slight banging noise. But that was nothing in comparison to the sound of the engine starting, which seemed loud enough to wake the dead. Quickly he put the car into reverse and backed out of the parking space until the passenger door was level with the gap that the children were still hidden in.

'Quick! Jump in,' he hissed at the children as he unlocked the passenger door and swung it open. By now he could see that some of the Moon Stealers had crawled along the carriage roof, drawn by the noise. A couple of them leapt over to the top of the station building and stared down at the car. Their eyes looked like several small lamps shining brightly in the night sky, searching for their prey.

The children didn't look back or hesitate, they just ran and dived through the open door as fast as they could. Edgar pushed against the accelerator so fast that the tires squealed as they spun against the tarmac as the car lurched forward. Scarlet hadn't had chance to close the passenger door behind her before the car moved, but as Edgar pulled the car to the left and out of the car park, the door swung shut and they drove away from the train as fast as they could.

Dark shapes began gathering in the sky above them, watching like an owl watches an unsuspecting mouse from afar.

30. ROSERY WOOD

Steven and Georgia followed the man with the shotgun into the cover of the trees and watched in horror as the dead bodies were feasted on by the skeletal black shadows. Steven kept his handgun ready to fire at an attacking creature should it come nearer to them, but they didn't seem to notice them from within the thick wooden trunks of the trees, concentrating on the curious people who came out of their houses to see what all the noise was about.

'Thanks for saving us back there,' said Steven in a breathless whisper. 'Who are you?'

'They call me Tracker; I'm the gamekeeper of these woods.'

Steven introduced himself and Georgia and made it appear that they were just in Parsley Bottom on holiday. Tracker looked down at the weapon in Steven's hand, a look of confusion passed over his face, but he decided not to ask about the gun.

'This is unbelievable. Have you ever seen anything like this before?' Tracker asked Steven. 'What do you think they are?' Now that they were closer to him, Steven noticed that his skin was well tanned and there was at least two days worth of golden stubble on his chin. He wore a blue baseball cap on his head that promoted an American baseball team that Steven had never heard of, and some golden straw coloured curls licked up from under the back of the cap around his neck. The cap cast a dark shadow over his eyes, but there still appeared to be a light green sparkle coming through as he stared over to them.

Without waiting for an answer he turned around and walked away, leaving Steven and Georgia no other choice but to follow behind. He walked at a quick pace and they both had to do a short burst of quicker steps to keep up with him.

'Where are we going?' shouted Steven to Tracker's retreating back.

'Into Rosary Woods,' came the reply. 'There are loads of those creatures in the sky as well as roaming the streets of Parsley Bottom. I tried to help as many people as I could but there's just too many of them. For now, the only way we can protect ourselves is to hide amongst the trees and wait for daylight.'

Steven felt uncomfortable about following an armed man that they didn't know and could be dangerous, away from civilisation and into woodland, but for now they didn't have any other option. He remembered that Coldred had said the creatures reacted badly to daylight and realised that they wouldn't be able to help many people while it was night.

'Do you know Rosery Woods?' Steven asked Georgia quietly.

'I've seen it on the map. It's woodland that forms part of the Butterwick Hall estate,' she whispered back to Steven.

'That's correct Miss,' shouted Tracker who had obviously still managed to hear them talking despite walking twelve feet ahead of them. The large trees towered high above them as they went deeper into the woodland. Tracker took out a torch and followed a path that had been well trodden so that no grass or weeds had chance to grow along it.

The thickened tree trunks in the woodland were old with brown dry bark that flaked off as they brushed against it. As they walked further amongst the trees the path became only wide enough for them to walk in single file and occasionally thorny brambles would snag and pull at their trousers or they would have to duck under a lower branch.

'Where are we going?' Steven asked once again.

Tracker stopped and turned round.

'I'm finding a way through the woodland to get us into the rear entrance of Butterwick Hall. We should be safe there until the morning.'

Steven still felt unsure about whether they had made the right decision to follow Tracker into such an isolated place, but if he had been a danger to them he could have easily left them to the creatures in Parsley Bottom.

After another couple of minutes walking they reached a glade that was surrounded by rocks on either side. They remained here watching the skies above for any sign of the creatures for several minutes. The trees on one side appeared to be thinner and they could see between the trunks and across the Yorkshire Moors.

'We need to get across this glade to get onto the paths that will take us to the Hall,' Tracker whispered to Steven and Georgia. 'There's this as well,' he added kicking at a blanket that was wedged between some rocks.

Steven walked nearer to the man. At his feet was a red and yellow tartan blanket, frayed at the edges with some holes worn in the middle. The blanket was weighed down at all four corners by heavy stones and it didn't appear to be lying smoothly against the ground. In the limited glow from the moon, it looked like there was something trapped beneath it and as he lifted one of the stones from the corner he pulled the fabric back to reveal the black skin of a creature.

The creature's body appeared to be in a sleeping position similar to that of a baby. Lying on its side with the arms folded to rest on the chest area below its head. At the end of each arm were two hooked claw like fingers together with a thin flap of black skin that hung lifelessly across where its back would be. Two long thin skeletal legs were also tucked up towards the body. Given more time, the creature Georgia had taken to London would have grown into a creature like this one once it was fully grown. It was almost like looking at an enlarged bat with longer arms and legs. The same singular milky white eye stared back at them and a hole beneath the eye hung slightly open to reveal a ring of small inward pointing teeth. There was also a large gun shot wound on its chest where the blackened skin had been lost to reveal a yellowy grey mass of tissue and flesh. At the edges of the wound and also forming a trail down to the ground was a crusty yellow liquid.

'Is it dead?' said Georgia as she took a step backwards. Steven nodded slowly.

'What happened?' Steven asked Tracker.

'I was making my way back from doing my evening checks of the perimeter when I saw something black hanging from that tree over there,' he pointed to a large oak tree on the edge of the glade. 'As I took a step nearer to it to see what it was, it flew into the air and swept down to attack me. I ducked just in time before it circled round to have another go. This time I was ready and shot it through the chest. From the edge of the woodland I could see a swarm of these creatures circling above the town, every now and again one would drop down like an eagle that had spotted its prey. There wasn't much that I could do on my own. One shotgun would not be able to stop their attack.'

'How many do you think there are?' asked Steven.

'I don't know, hundreds I suppose.'

Steven sat on the dewy grass next to the creature thinking about what to do next. There was no point in going back to town to try and stop the creatures from attacking the rest of the people. It wouldn't be long before they too became victims to them or ran out of ammunition. The best thing he could think of was to wait until daylight. If the creatures were more vulnerable in the daylight, they may hide themselves away and he might still be able to find the nest then call in the SWAT team as Seward and Coldred had instructed.

'Could we take the body somewhere?' Steven asked Tracker.

'Why? Shouldn't we just burn it?'

'No. This is an animal that we haven't met before and it needs studying carefully. If they're killing humans we need to find out how to stop them or at least how to protect ourselves against them.'

'Who are you?' Tracker asked Steven once again, 'and this time the truth. No one on holiday carries a handgun with them when they go out for an evening stroll.'

'We work for MI6 and we need to get this body back to London.'

'There's too many of these things out there. We wouldn't get far.'

'What about if we store it somewhere,' Georgia asked, 'then after we've gone into Parsley Bottom in daylight we could retrieve the car and take it to London.'

Tracker thought about it. 'There's an old Ice House in the grounds of Butterwick Hall. The cold would stop it from deteriorating.'

'What's an Ice House?' Georgia asked.

'It's what they used before refrigerators where invented. It's a brick building where ice would have been stored underground so that food could be kept fresher for longer.'

Steven and Tracker wrapped the creature in the blanket and began dragging it behind them as they cautiously walked into the glade. Silently Tracker directed them across to the other side, constantly checking the sky for more creatures until they safely reached the other side of the clearing. Ahead of them Steven could see a small lake that swept round some trees to the left, but then he caught a glimpse of something dark flash across the surface of the water.

Suddenly, Tracker stopped.

Steven took a few more steps forward before he realised that Tracker was no longer walking beside him. Georgia, who had been walking behind the two men had also stopped next to Tracker

'Don't move. We're being watched,' he said without moving his head. He was listening closely to the sounds in the wood. The sounds he knew so well were now different, the sound of the wind between the trees had changed; the sound of animals snuffling through the undergrowth had stopped. Tracker looked over to Steven, 'There are at least four of those creatures in the trees above us.' Very slowly Tracker reached to his belt and took two shotgun cartridges out and slid them into the barrels of the gun.

'You might need that gun now,' he said to Steven as they both suddenly became aware of a breathy gurgling sound coming from above. It was heading straight down towards them and at speed.

31. THE ICE HOUSE

There was a whistling sound in the air above them as something heavy sank quickly towards the ground. In one swift action Tracker, who was alert to the changes in the wood, looked up to the sky and released a cartridge from his shotgun into the black shape that was coming straight towards him. A hole instantly appeared in the wing of the creature causing it to spin and twist uncontrollably, skimming low before crashing into a tree and falling into a pile of leaves at the base. The blast from the gun knocked Tracker backwards until he stumbled and fell so that he was now lying down looking up towards the canopy of the trees and the remaining creatures that circled in the sky above them. Steven had hesitated but now he pulled the gun out from the back of his trousers and crept over to Tracker to help him up off the ground. Georgia also had gone over to Tracker and was crouched down on the floor keeping out of the way of the guns.

Tracker watched the other three creatures above them, two more now started to plummet to the ground ready for another attack. Steven and Tracker both knelt down on the ground and supported their guns with both hands to keep themselves steady. Steven fired several bullets into the air, the sound echoing around the trees. Tracker didn't fire. At the sound of Steven's gun the creatures seemed to pull up out of their dive just skimming over the tops of their heads, but it didn't take long before they turned and came back round for another try, this time from opposite directions. Steven fired again and he knew that at least a couple of bullets had punctured the wings of the creature that came towards him, but the holes were not as big as those caused by the shotgun and the creature continued to glide unharmed towards him. Steven knew that he needed to aim at the head if he wanted to kill the creature, so watched calmly and carefully along the barrel of the gun until he could clearly see the eye of the creature. He squeezed the trigger and another bullet span out of the barrel and pieced the white eye. The creature's body now limp and heavy, was carried by the speed and momentum it had built up in flight and tumbled straight into Steven and Georgia, knocking them backwards onto Tracker.

Tracker had also been taking his time to aim carefully at the creature as it came towards him, but as Steven and Georgia knocked into him, the round from his gun shot harmlessly into the ground. The creature skimmed over the heads of Steven and Georgia, its hooked claws trailing down as it flew over, cutting into the soft flesh of Steven's chest. Steven let out a sharp yell as two lines of blood quickly appeared through the torn material of his shirt. He rolled onto the leafy ground, the gun harmlessly tossed under a bramble bush, as the pain across his chest burnt and stung.

Tracker knew that they couldn't move to safety yet and could see the creature that had just scratched Steven had now already turned and started its dive back towards them. He refilled the shotgun whilst all the time keeping the creature in his sights and calmly waited for it to come closer. Near to Steven a black figure had now lifted itself from the base of a tree and was moving awkwardly towards Steven. It was the first creature that Tracker had shot through the wing and as it could no longer fly straight, it was ready to resume its attack from the ground. The crash into the tree must have damaged it in other ways as it was dragging one leg behind it and partially pulling itself with its arms and the hooked fingers slowly across the ground. Georgia rushed over to Steven, picked up a fallen branch from one of the trees and swung it as hard as she could into the side of the creature's head. The branch exploded into many pieces showering Steven in wooden splinters. The creature seemed to twist in the air, lifted off the ground by the force of the strike to land motionless back on the ground. At the same time she heard Tracker's gun go off with a loud echoing boom that repeated itself as it bounced from tree to tree far into the distance. There was silence for two seconds before it was followed by a dull thump and a rustling sound made by something heavy skimming across the ground into a dead heap.

Tracker skidded over to Steven and Georgia, keeping a careful eye on the sky above. There was one more creature circling above, but it didn't look like it was getting ready to attack. Suddenly a piercing screeching noise cut through the air making Georgia cover her ears. Whether the sound was in sorrow for the fallen creatures they weren't sure, but Tracker had a feeling that it was more likely a call for help and guessed that reinforcements would soon be on their way.

'Quick, we have to move,' he said forcefully to Georgia. 'Help him up; the Ice House is not far, it's the nearest place for shelter. They know we're here. We've got to move!'

With Tracker holding Steven under one arm and Georgia under the other, they both managed to lift him off the ground and stagger forward with him along the path. Steven had to walk with his back bent forward because every time he stood up straight, the wound would open once again and pain would shoot through his chest.

The three of them stumbled together along the path until the trees cleared and they came out alongside the lake. Around the edges of the lake there were muddy banks with tree trunks clinging to the soil, their thick roots exposed but somehow succeeding in keeping the tree from falling into the water. All the time they walked, Tracker kept his shotgun raised towards the sky, keeping a careful eye on the remaining creature as it watched them from its perch in the top of the trees. No further attacks happened but the creature continued to make more piercing calls waiting for other creatures to arrive.

The path through the woodland now joined onto a better tended path edged with wood to hold the earth back and was covered with a sandy gravel. This was harder for Steven to stumble across as his feet slid on the loose gravel, but luckily he was starting to get over the shock of the attack and although the wound on his chest still stung he was starting to gain his strength back.

As the path wound alongside the lake the ground to the left of the path became more raised and they eventually reached a small brick-lined opening that cut into a mound of earth. Georgia was surprised to see a brick arch with a thick wooden door built into the earth, almost like it was the entrance to someone's house. On top of the mound moss had grown, but occasionally the surface of a brick domed roof could still be seen where the soil and moss had been washed away.

'This is the Ice House,' said Tracker as he propped Steven against one of the sloped brick walls that held the earth back from the entrance.

At that point a loud chorus of screeching could be heard in the distance, answered by the remaining creature that had been watching them as they walked along the path. Steven and Georgia quickly turned around and could see a dark cloud coming across the top of the trees in the distance. It moved quickly and as it got nearer the cloud seemed to separate into numerous black shaped creatures, their leathery wings flapping rapidly like a swarm of bats. The creature that had survived the earlier attack now leapt from its perch on the top of one of the trees and was circling in the air above the Ice House.

The creatures turned rapidly towards them.

'Quick, we better get under cover,' Tracker said desperately to Georgia.

Tracker handed the shotgun to Steven while he quickly took a bundle of keys out of his pocket and started to sort through them trying to find the right one for the lock. The large ring held many different sizes and shapes of keys and Tracker was now trying them all individually inside the rusty lock in the door. The now familiar sound of wind rushing towards them began again as the creatures started to dive at them once more. The mound of earth gave them some protection from the sides and back so the creatures were unable to dive down as close to them as they had done in the woods, but still they kept swooping. Tracker continued to try the keys until finally one of them slotted into the lock and he could turn it, but it had been many years since the Ice House had been opened and the rust had fused the door stiff. Tracker repeatedly pushed with his shoulder trying to loosen the door from the frame. With every attack from above, the creatures seemed to be getting nearer and nearer. Steven and Georgia pushed themselves as close as they could to the door of the Ice House, Georgia instinctively ducking every time one of the creatures came near.

Suddenly they all became aware of a different sound other than the air sweeping and whooshing around them. There was a breathy gurgling sound coming from above them, but not in the air. As they all looked up they stared straight into the moon like eye of a creature that had landed on top of the mound of earth and was perched on the ground high above the brick arch that went round the door. It clawed at them with one arm whilst holding itself steady with the other over the arch of the door frame. They all managed to dodge the claw as it came for a second grab at them.

Georgia screamed.

Whilst their attention had focused on the creature above them they hadn't noticed that some of the others had now started to land on the path in front of them. Another creature was now slowly walking towards them, using its legs and the claws on its wings for balance, whilst the attack continued from the sky. They had nowhere to go; they were trapped between a brick wall on either side and a door behind them. All around were creatures, possibly thirty or forty, some on the ground and some still in the air. Steven felt the cold steel of the trigger of the shotgun underneath his finger and he remembered that he still had a chance for survival. At least he could kill a few more of these creatures before they got to them.

He levelled the shotgun at the creature approaching them on the path and pulled the trigger. The force of the shotgun pellets knocked the creature off its feet and a pool of yellow liquid erupted from the hole in the middle of its chest. As he had pulled the trigger, the force of the gun pushed him backwards against the door which gave it the push it needed to release it from its rusty frame and open into the Ice House. Tracker, who had been pushing against the door with his shoulder, stumbled forward but the other two who were facing the other way fell backwards and were now lying on the floor half in the Ice House and half out of it. The creature on the roof jumped down and was now standing where Steven and Georgia had just been. Steven let off another shot from the gun knocking the creature backwards. They then scrabbled backwards while Tracker pushed the door back into its frame.

The last shot from the gun had made a deafening sound inside the Ice House and all they could now hear was a ringing in their ears. As Tracker found the key to lock the door, it was suddenly pushed inwards, knocking him once more to the floor. In the doorway stood two of the creatures silhouetted against the night sky scratching their clawed hands on the ground. Although Steven saw Georgia's mouth open in a scream, all he could hear was the ringing from the gun blast. Instinctively all three of them jumped up and ran at the door pushing it with all their combined strength and forcing it against the creatures to push it into the frame while Tracker turned the lock.

They all sat exhausted on the floor gasping for breath as they took the stale air of the Ice House into their lungs. All they could hear was the ringing in their ears and the thumping of their hearts as it quickly pushed blood around their bodies. Inside the Ice House it was pitch black. Slowly the ringing got less and they became aware of banging and scratching on the outside of the door as well as gentle thuds from above as more creatures landed on the roof of the building.

Tracker reached to his belt and took out a pocket flashlight which he shone over to Steven and Georgia then checked the area around him. Hanging on the wall beside the inner door he saw a storm lamp which he removed. Striking a match he lit the lamp, hoping there was still some paraffin inside. A warm orange glow filled the chamber.

'Let's move through into the next chamber,' Tracker instructed as he pointed to the second internal door.

Again Tracker worked his way through the keys until he found the one that opened the door and they entered another chamber. Here the air was even damper and old, like it had been trapped inside the building for years. Locking the door behind them, they now had two barriers between themselves and the creatures. This chamber was a lot cooler than the first. Tracker moved the lamp over to Steven so that he could check his wounds. Georgia took a bottle of water and a clean paper napkin from her bag and used it to clean Steven's wounds.

They stood and looked around their surroundings. Apart from the area they were currently in, there was a red brick chamber which had some steps leading down to the bottom and was dominated by a large circular dome roof. Tracker swung the lamp down.

'This is where the ice used to be put to keep this chamber cold. There's a small drainage hole at the bottom that leads out to the lake,' he told Steven and Georgia.

'Apart from the drain and the doorway, are there any other ways the creatures could get in?' asked Georgia with a nervous quiver in her voice.

'No,' replied Tracker.

'But there's also no other way for us to get out,' added Steven sarcastically, his face strained and bloody.

'So what are we going to do?' Georgia asked in a panic.

'Stay calm,' Tracker said forcefully. 'Let's just sit and wait. While we recover from the attack we can work out what to do next. You never know, they may give up and leave us alone.'

The persistent bangs and scratches on the main entrance door could still be heard from inside the second chamber as well as the muffled, but still high pitched screams of the creatures. Tracker turned his light off to save the paraffin.

They sat down and waited nervously in the dark.

32. ONE WAY OUT

As the night progressed the thuds and bangs of the creatures trying to get into the ice house continued. So far the entrance door with its rusty lock had managed to hold up.

'How are we going to get out of here?' asked Steven from inside the darkness.

He could hear his two companions breathing from either side of him and could tell which was which by sniffing the air around him; the sweet fragrant perfume of Georgia that he had got used to during the last couple of days was on his left, whilst on the right, there was a heavier smell of Tracker that reminded Steven of the smell of overly dry earth after a shower of rain.

'I'm not sure,' replied Tracker after a while, 'but that door might not stay secure for too much longer. They're certainly persistent creatures.'

'If this old building is built of bricks, couldn't we try taking some of them out and escape through the roof?' Georgia suggested, her voice echoing inside the enclosed chamber.

'If the creatures are still outside they would soon be able to jump onto the roof and get into the Ice House through the hole we're trying to create before we had a chance to get out, ' he paused, 'No. The only way out is through the front door.'

Except for the bangs outside, there was a peaceful silence inside the darkened building but sitting on the floor where they were was starting to make them feel quite cold. Without warning a light appeared from the dark casting a yellow glow around the chamber, Tracker had lit a match and was trying to ignite the Storm Lamp. The sudden change of light caused them all to squint and screw their eyes up but they soon adjusted to the change from the darkness.

'What do you think we should do?' asked Steven.

'We need to head towards Butterwick Hall. It's not far from here, just a short walk from the lake. It would probably take about three minutes walking, but maybe just one minute if we ran. When we get inside, there are food stores as well as more weapons.'

'Is it secure?'

'It should be. It's an old house, so all the windows are made up of small leaded squares, the doors are thick wooden ones, reinforced with steel hinges and studs. It's not a fortress but it's better than being in here,' Tracker said. 'What's in your bag?' he added addressing Georgia.

She unzipped the bag and emptied the contents onto the floor at their feet. As well as the other handgun, additional ammunition and boxes of antibiotics, there was her purse, some test tube shaped sample bottles, car keys and a make up bag.

'Where's your car?' asked Tracker.

'Not far from where you saw us. It's parked outside the Fox and Hound Pub in the village,' she replied.

Tracker picked the make up bag off the floor and looked inside it. He pulled a travel size aerosol deodorant can out of the bag and shook it close to his ear so that he could hear how much was left inside. It seemed to Tracker that it was a fairly new can considering the weight of it.

'How accurate are you at shooting?' he asked Steven, 'Have you ever been clay pigeon shooting?'

'No, but I'm fairly good.'

'This aerosol can could be our way out of here. Aerosols are made of compressed air and contain gases that burn and explode easily. If we threw the can outside and shot it, the explosion may injure a few of the creatures, but the main effect would be shock and that might just give us enough time to get out of here and run for the main house.'

'But we would have to open the entrance door to do it,' said Steven, 'we'd only get one chance. Maybe you should take the shot at the can rather than me,' he told Tracker, unsure in his own ability with the gun.

'I'm happy to take the shot, but I will need your gun to do it. You would need to cover me with the shotgun.' Tracker loaded the last two shots into his shotgun and clicked the barrels back into place.

Georgia packed everything back into her bag including the additional cases of bullets for Steven's gun and firmly pulled the straps over both shoulders.

'Well, there's no time like the present,' said Tracker cheerfully.

Georgia took the lamp from Tracker whilst he found the keys again and unlocked the inner door to the chamber. Although they could still hear the scratching at the outer door and knew that the smaller chamber between the two doors would be safe, they still cautiously opened the door by a small crack, guns at the ready and checked that it was secure before moving into the section behind the outer door. They could see that splinters of wood had been scratched away from the sides as well as the base of the door and the dark shadows of the creatures moving around outside could be seen silhouetted against the night. Georgia placed the lamp on the floor and took the bunch of keys from Tracker. He held one of the keys out separately to the others so that she knew which one was the key to the outer door. The three of them moved slowly towards the door trying not to be put off by the sound of the claws scratching or the wet rasping breath that was coming from the other side.

'We all need to be ready to protect ourselves from the explosion so we need to keep pressed up against this door to prevent the blast from pushing it in,' whispered Tracker to the other two who nodded. Georgia carefully and quietly slid the key into the keyhole ready to turn it when the time was right. Tracker had now begun examining the holes that had been made around the door, one of which, below a hinge was big enough for him to shoot through. At the base of the door, chunks of wood had splintered and been torn away, he reached down to place the aerosol can on the floor just on the inside of the door but lined up with the hole. He jumped back with fright as long clawed fingers poked in under the door towards the can and began scratching two deep lines into the dry ground. Tracker stamped his heavy booted foot down onto the fingers which resulted in a high pitched scream from the creature at the door, but the fingers quickly got pulled back. Tracker put the can nearer to the hole then kicked it through with the toe of his boot. He quickly then looked out of the hole near the hinge and raised the gun so that he could shoot it, but couldn't see where it had gone. Some of the creatures had now moved away from the door and over to the right hand side of the path distracted and drawn towards the can.

'I can't get a clear shot at the can,' he whispered to the others. Georgia's hand was held tightly around the door key ready to turn whilst Steven held the shotgun in both hands, his back pressed firmly against the door.

The sound of bricks falling behind them echoed from inside the large chamber of the Ice House near to where they had been sitting.

'We have to hurry!' whispered Georgia, 'they must be starting to break through the roof!'

'Can you see the aerosol yet?' Steven asked Tracker impatiently as the sound of a larger number of bricks crashed into the bottom of the chamber.

Feeling the need for urgency, Tracker decided to create a diversion to move some of the creatures away from the can so that he could see it to shoot it clearly. He carefully looked straight down the barrel of the gun and aimed it at a creature that was on the outside of the gathering of creatures. As he pulled the trigger and released a bullet into the head of the creature the bang of the gun was also mixed with the heavy thud of a creature as it jumped down from the hole in the roof behind them and landed at the bottom of the deeper chamber of the ice house. It wouldn't take long for it to climb out and attack them from within. Outside the creature that had been shot had fallen to the floor and the rest of the group had instinctively flown away like a flock of frightened birds. By the side of the dead creature Tracker could now see the violet purple coloured canister of deodorant lying on the ground. As it had spun to rest it pointed away from the Ice House, so the most that he could see was the base of it and a small amount of one of the sides. He knew that the creatures wouldn't have flown far away and were probably waiting in a tree or further along the path. They wouldn't stand a chance if they tried to run for the house without the element of surprise. If he was going to shoot the can it would have no effect if the creatures were at a safe distance, he needed to tempt them back before the one that had now got into the chamber came through and attacked them from inside. Tracker thought quickly.

'Use that key and lock the inner door,' he instructed to Georgia.

'But we'll be trapped between these two doors!'

'Do it and do it quick, it sounds like there's a creature in the chamber and it will soon be making its way towards us. I'm not ready to be breakfast just yet!'

Georgia stepped away from the door and slotted the key into the inner door and locked it. They were now sandwiched between two wooden doors with creatures on both sides.

'Take off your shirt,' Tracker said to Steven, 'we need to tempt them back so that the explosion from the can will be effective.'

Steven nodded, understanding that the blood on his shirt would draw the creatures back towards the Ice House entrance. He pulled it over his head and wiped it on his chest, although the blood had now started to clot it still left streaks of red across the material.

'The creature from the chamber is right behind this door,' said Georgia who was still standing next to the inner door, 'I can hear it breathing against the wood.'

'Get ready to open the door,' Tracker indicated the main entrance door to Georgia, 'just enough so Steven can throw the shirt out, but close and lock it immediately.'

Georgia moved towards the outer door. She knew that this was the only way that they could escape from the Ice House and she knew what waited for them outside. Her hand hesitated on the key inside the lock; part of her didn't dare unlock it. Her hand felt rigid and solid like she didn't have any control over it. She took a deep breath and began twisting the key taking every bit of strength she could find. The rusty metal lock slid out of the frame and the weight of the thick wooden door made it swing slightly towards them. Steven rolled up his shirt and threw it towards the left side of the path so that it wasn't in front of the aerosol can. Georgia then pushed the door back into its frame and locked it again. Almost immediately three creatures dived onto the shirt from the roof of the Ice House, followed by several more from the sky. Steven picked up the shotgun he had laid on the floor. There was now scratching coming from the other side of the inner door.

'Ready?' said Tracker to the other two. He had been pointing the gun through the gap under the hinge of the door for several minutes so far, but now that the time was upon him, he started to question whether or not he would be able to shoot the small canister. All those times as a child that he had missed clay pigeons when out shooting with his father came flooding back to him. He felt like he was a skinny uncoordinated teenager once again, scared of being an embarrassment to his father in front of his friends. Tracker held the gun firmly in the palm of his hand and pulled the trigger back. The bullet spun out of the barrel and almost immediately an explosion ripped through the air outside causing the door to rattle in its frame.

Georgia unlocked the door once again and they sprang out into the open air. A blackened mark now showed where the can had been on the path and a lot of the gravel had been forced away from the explosion. The bodies of some of the creatures that had been nearest to the can lay on the path, whilst others seemed to be wounded and were limping or rolling on the ground. Georgia looked around her nervously whilst following Tracker and Steven as they ran away from the Ice House. Although the explosion had given them the opportunity to get out of the Ice House, it didn't take the creatures long to regroup and Georgia could see that some of the creatures that were furthest from the blast were starting to flap their wings and lift off the ground ready to pursue them.

33. THE MAGIC PORTAL

Edgar drove the car as fast as he could along the roads. He seemed to know where he was going and the children held on tightly as they took the corners at speed, the tires occasionally squealing as the rubber tried desperately to grip onto the road surface. Scarlet sat in the passenger seat next to Edgar whilst the two boys were in the back, sliding from one side to the other.

'Whose car is this?' asked Scarlet in a loud voice over the revving hum of the engine.

'I don't know, but he won't be using it any more,' replied Edgar as he looked in the rear view mirror. He was sure that they were being followed by some of the Moon Stealers as he kept catching glimpses of black shapes flying in the sky above them. Luckily there didn't appear to be any other cars on the road although Edgar still had to avoid ones that had been abandoned at awkward angles beside the road. Some cars appeared to have been driven down into the ditch with only their exhaust pipes sticking up into the air.

There was a heavy thud from the roof of the car. Scarlet screamed and jumped in her seat. Edgar quickly glanced up and saw that the metal of the roof was now bent down in several places from whatever the falling object had been. Something had managed to land on the top of the moving car and Edgar had a pretty good idea what it was. He swerved the car from left to right, jerking it from one side of the road to the other, trying to shake the creature from the roof. In one of the side mirrors he saw a black creature tumble from the top of the car and land against the side of a parked car, leaving a large dent in the metal work and causing the orange lights of the car alarm to flash repeatedly.

'Phew, that was close,' said Joe as he watched the creature out of the back window.

'Look out!' shouted Max to Edgar. He was pointing towards the front windscreen. Lit up by the headlights of the car was a Moon Stealer standing directly in the middle of the road, both it's arms outstretched, the wings hanging down, it's small round mouth open in a menacing way. Edgar didn't try to stop or swerve out of the way; instead he put his foot down even harder on the accelerator and lined the car up with the creature. As they got nearer and nearer the children covered their eyes with their hands. Edgar drove the car straight into the Moon Stealer. The car jolted at the impact, a splatter of fluid covered the car and yellow liquid now smeared the front windscreen. Edgar turned on the wipers and squirted the windscreen with the water jets and quickly the glass was clear again so that he could see the road ahead.

Another metallic thud echoed from the roof of the car. The roof was starting to become a lot lower than it originally had been and was bent in the middle, meaning Joe and Max could not keep their heads upright. This time claws appeared at both sides of the car clamping the Moon Stealer tightly on. This creature would be harder to shake off than the first.

Edgar had noticed that the paint on the bonnet of the car was beginning to blister and bubble from the acidic fluid that had covered the car when he drove into the Moon Stealer. He continued to drive as fast as he could as they entered Parsley Bottom along Harrogate Road past Manor Cottage, then swung the car hard to the right and into a smaller lane. From where they were the town appeared deserted. Although there were a few lights on in the houses there was no one in sight. Some wisps of grey smoke rose into the air from several places within the town which didn't appear to be coming from house chimneys, but from abandoned cars.

'What's happened?' said Max with a tone of sadness in his voice.

'We must go on,' replied Edgar firmly, 'or we will end up the same as everyone that was on the train.'

Edgar did not hesitate or slow the car, but continued past the church and followed the lane up the hill along the road between two fields of farmland. They drove over a small bridge, which caused the car to leap slightly into the air, before continuing towards the Faerie Ring at the top of the hill.

As Edgar pulled the car to a standstill, the tires skidding on loose dirt on the road surface, he opened the door and drew his sword in one swift movement. Before the creature on the roof had chance to jump off, Edgar had detached its head from the rest of the body and was running round to the passenger door. He could see the dark shapes of more Moon Stealers in the sky above them. Scarlet had had already opened the passenger door and was starting to climb out.

'Don't touch the car!' shouted Edgar to the children, 'stay very close to me. Come on!'

Edgar started running up the path, through the gate towards the stone circle silhouetted against the sky. Moon Stealers swept down towards them, but something magical seemed to be seeping out from the point of Edgar's sword as he held it above them chanting something that none of the children understood. There appeared to be a white shimmering shield of light that was arced above their heads, protecting them from the creatures as they dived down to attack. They seemed to be repelled by the shield of light that Edgar's sword was creating, bouncing harmlessly back into the sky.

'Joe!' instructed Edgar between his chanting, 'get the Silver Bough ready! As soon as we enter the inside of the Faerie Ring start blowing into it.'

'But what do I play!' said Joe who instinctively ducked as another Moon Stealer hit the shield above his head.

'The Bough will know. All you need to do is blow into it!' The shield had begun to get smaller in size as Edgar spoke to Joe. 'Don't hesitate. The sword's magic won't last for much longer.'

The tall stones of the circle were now directly in front of them. They raced through the outer stones and stood in the centre next to the stones of Gawain and Belphoebe. They all formed a circle themselves facing out watching the Moon Stealers as they swam in the air above their heads. Joe removed the Silver Bough from the cloth, its surface shone in the dark of the night. Soft music filled the air, surrounding them all in a comforting blanket of sound.

'Blew into it Joe!' said Edgar urgently as the shield of light got so small that it vanished into the tip of the sword. Joe put the cold metal pipe to his lips and blew. Sweet sounds like hollow bells and metallic vibrations came out of the bottom of the pipe.

As Joe continued to blow into the pipe two Moon Stealers had landed on the ground and were now advancing towards them. Edgar stood between the children and the Moon Stealers, sword ready to attack. Small lines of white smoke began to form between the two standing stones of Gawain and Belphoebe, appearing to circle from one central point and slowly spin outwards leaving behind a thin ghostly cloud. It rippled and moved like it was a shimmering pool of water. Joe continued to blow faster, encouraged by what he saw forming in front of him, making the portal grow even bigger. The pool of water appeared to be standing upright against all laws of gravity and despite its mirrored surface the stones behind it could still be seen.

The Moon Stealers continued to advance towards them.

Edgar moved forward and swung Ethera at the first Moon Stealer, plunging the sword deep into the creatures' chest. A splash of acidic juices dripped from Edgar's sword onto his hand, he cried out in pain, as a small patch of flesh began dissolving before his eyes. Glancing behind him he could see that the portal was ready.

'Go!' he shouted to the children.

'But what about my family,' Max shouted.

Scarlet firmly gripped hold of Max and Joe's hands and together they leapt through the open portal.

As soon as they had gone the shimmering pool began to shrink.

Edgar was now on his own.

He quickly swung his sword to detach the arm of a Moon Stealer that was attempting to grab him, followed by a desperate two handed swing that cut straight through the creature's shoulder and into its neck. He turned and leapt at the shrinking portal just before it sucked into itself leaving the Faerie Ring empty once again.

Dark shadows continued to circle from above, but for tonight at least, Edgar and the children weren't going to be another victim of the Moon Stealers.

34. ESCAPE TO BUTTERWICK HALL

Steven, Georgia and Tracker ran as fast as they could along the gravel path beside the lake and rounded a small collection of trees so that they were now facing the back of Butterwick Hall. Steven looked up into the night sky at the circling black shadows of the creatures that were now approaching them from above the house and diving out of the sky towards them. Several creatures swept towards Tracker making him dive to the ground, but Steven was ready. He had already knelt down onto one knee and was levelling the shotgun at the leader of the group. Shotgun pellets burst into the group, scattering them in different directions. The creature he shot fell down to the ground, knocking another creature out of the sky as it dropped.

Tracker picked himself off the ground. With their heads bent low Steven and Georgia went over to join him. Georgia was watching from behind and could see more creatures from around the Ice House joining the others ready to attack from the air behind them.

'Come on,' called Tracker, 'we must get to the house! There's too many of them.'

As the bodies of the creatures swept down towards them they continued to run towards the back area of the house. Steven could see that there was an entrance door to the left of the building that was obviously the servants' wing. The door appeared to be open. All they had to do was head towards it. Although they would feel safer inside the house, it would only be a short term measure based on the destructive force they had seen the creatures perform. But it would give them time to think of a plan, as well as collect extra weapons and food.

In front of them was a well manicured lawn which felt soft and spongy beneath their feet. Steven instinctively ducked his head and twisted behind him to see the white cloudy eye of a creature bearing down on him. He swung his gun round and released his final barrel of pellets into the air above his head. There was a small explosion from the creature's body which caused a yellow fluid to shower the grass around them as they continued to run towards the house.

'I'm out of bullets!' shouted Steven to Tracker. Georgia let out a scream as one of the creatures began lifting her away from the ground by the claws it had hooked into the bag over her shoulders. Tracker took aim and shot two bullets into the creature which fell to the ground along with Georgia. They were only a short distance from the door. Steven and Tracker lifted Georgia under her arms and ran with her the final stretch of the grass, onto the gravel towards the door. Suddenly a creature landed on the gravel in front of the door blocking their way in. Tracker raised his gun once again and shot what bullets he had left directly into the eye of the creature whilst still running forward. Behind them more black shapes fell from the sky as Tracker helped Georgia leap over the body of the creature that had fallen in front of the door. As soon as they were all through the doorway, Steven swung the barrel of the shotgun to hit the side of a creature's face that had approached them from behind, then all three pushed the door into the stone archway, sealing the creatures outside. They leant against the door as hard as they could to prevent the creatures from getting in whilst Tracker sorted through the keys. Every now and again they felt the thud of creatures bang against the door, jarring their backs forward, until Tracker managed to lock the door. He then reached up and pushed a bolt at the top of the door into the stone wall then did the same at the bottom.

Together they sank down onto the floor, panting. Georgia could feel the blood being pushed forcefully around her body, could hear her heart beat inside her ears and feel her chest thumping. Although the bangs continued against the door, they knew that they were safe for now.

A smash came from the side of the door and a blackened claw hooked through the shards of glass.

Tracker leapt to his feet, picking up a spade that was propped up against a wall and swung it down hard onto the skeletal hand that was desperately trying to claw its way inside.

'We need to get away from the windows and doors and make sure they are secure,' he said, 'let's stay together.'

The three of them first started in the room they had just entered, pushing furniture and tables up against the windows. They left some of them that were too small to pose a danger before following Tracker through into the neighbouring rooms. Tracker collected keys as they went through the house, locking the doors behind them. After checking the kitchen and the rest of the servant's wing they made their way into the grander part of the house, moving thick solid furniture to bar the doors and windows.

The dining room looked out from the front of the house towards the gravel driveway with its shallow fountain. The room had dark wood panelling at both ends, decorated with gold ornate framed paintings and carved shields with crossed swords behind. In the centre a long oak table stretched the length of the room and to the side opposite the front windows a large stone engraved fire surround dominated the room. The table and fire didn't look like they had been used for some time as both were empty, with no cutlery on the table and no logs in the fireplace. Steven and Tracker automatically went up to the windows and checked that each lock was secure, whilst Georgia strolled over and admired the paintings, one of which showed a man dressed smartly in a suit outside the front of Butterwick Hall who seemed to closely resemble Tracker. Suddenly her attention was drawn towards the fireplace. She didn't know why, but something had caught her eye. A small movement or something out of place, she didn't know what it had been. Standing perfectly still she then noticed what it was that had got her attention, two hooks had appeared inside the fireplace underneath the mantelpiece and small trails of soot were falling silently from inside the chimney.

'Tracker,' she whispered to the Gamekeeper who had by now walked the length of the room to the opposite end to Georgia. He turned to her then followed her gaze towards the fireplace. A second set of hooks had now appeared and they could hear some soft movement from behind the wall space above the fireplace.

Tracker slipped the gun from between his trousers and his belt and aimed it at the fireplace. Steven climbed onto a chair that was probably priceless and pulled one of the swords from its display mount on the wall. They both walked slowly towards the fireplace as two clawed feet landed on the base. At first the creature looked smaller than the rest they had already encountered, but they soon realised that to get down the chimney, it had curled itself up with only the claws to grip onto the loose sooty sides. It now stretched itself up to its full height and unfolded its wings. The black curtain of an eyelid slowly lifted to reveal the white globe of an eye. Tracker pulled the trigger on his gun, but all it did was click harmlessly; he had run out of bullets during their escape to the house. Realising what had happened Steven ran round the table and charged forward with his antique sword. He swung his arms back ready to bring the sword into the creature but before he could, the creature let out a high pitched scream, flapped its wings and leapt onto the oak table. Steven missed and harmlessly struck the fireplace with the sword. Tracker leapt onto the chair and pulled the other sword from the wall together with the shield and began to advance towards the creature from the other side of the table. He swung at the creature's leg whilst deflecting an arm that clawed at him with the shield. As the creature's focus was on Tracker, Steven swung his sword at the other leg. Although the creature moved the leg out of the way, the tip of the sword slashed into the blackened flesh causing the creature to stumble forward slightly. In anger it swept its wing backwards and knocked Steven against the fire place, his head banging slightly against the stone surround. Using one of its long arms for support the creature managed to move along the table whilst still using its other arm to swing at Tracker. Once again, Tracker's shield deflected some blows from the creature but the continual force knocked him off balance and he stumbled backwards. The creature took its opportunity and leapt onto Tracker, the body weight of the creature pinning him to the ground so that he was unable to swing his sword at the creature. To Tracker's amazement it seemed like the creature was sweating, he could see small beads of liquid forming over its thick blackened skin. Where the creature's body was touching the shield, the metal now seemed to be smoking and there was an acidic smell in the air. The creature's face was just inches from Tracker, its stale breath blew from the small circular mouth below the eye. Suddenly the creature's body became even heavier as Tracker realised that it was no longer moving and no more air was coming out of the mouth. Confused, he tried to look round the body of the creature to see what had happened, but couldn't so stayed where he was. Georgia came into view and pushed at the creature with her foot to try and free him. It rolled off Tracker's body and crashed against some of the chairs. It was then that he noticed that the creature appeared to have a metal candle stick holder sticking out from its body.

'Thank you,' he said to Georgia as she helped to lift him off the ground. He examined the shield which was now useless as the surface was scarred and partially melted from the creature's attack.

A moaning noise now came from the fireplace and Tracker braced himself for another attack, but was relieved to see Steven standing up holding the back of his head from the knock he had received.

Between them they managed to tip the table on its side and push it against the fireplace to prevent any other creatures from entering the house through the chimney.

They continued to work methodically through the house locking all the doors they could and confining themselves to the lower floor servant's quarters which had very few, but small, windows, as well as a well stocked kitchen and the gamekeeper's weapons cupboard.

They sat in the kitchen nervously eating bread and cheese with swords and numerous loaded guns laid out across the thick oak table top ready to defend themselves should they need to. They took it in turns to stay awake and keep watch whilst the other two slept. The silence in the house would occasionally be broken by the thud of a creature as it attempted to break in.

By morning, with the presence of daylight, Steven hoped that the attack would have eased.

35. A MESSAGE FROM AFAR

Steven stretched his legs as he woke early the next morning. It took him a few seconds to remember what had happened during the night but it soon flooded back to him. He then sat silently listening, waiting for any sign that the creatures were still attacking the house, but apart from the heavy breathing of Georgia and Tracker, the house was silent. Georgia was slumped over the kitchen table, her head resting on top of her arms, whilst Tracker sat on his own in a single armchair in the corner with his shotgun across his knees.

He stood and walked around the kitchen, stopped at a cupboard where he took out some bread and butter, then found some strawberry jam in another cupboard. Standing eating a thick wedge of bread he noticed a small battery operated radio. He turned it on but all he could hear was static crackling from the speaker. Looking round the radio he found the tuning knob and started to rotate it. As he moved it from one piece of static to another, a whistling noise indicated the change in frequency but all he could pick up was the fuzz of static. Steven didn't think anything of this, after all radios often had difficulty picking up stations in different areas of the country, but then he came across a clearer gap in the static where a voice was coming out of the silence. He had to turn the volume up as loud as it would go to be able to hear it clearly. The voice was deep and rough with an American accent and seemed to almost growl from inside the radio.

'Last night the human race was attacked. Many people have already died and many others are, we believe, trapped or in hiding. If anyone can hear this message come and join us. We are a small band of survivors in London. Our strength is in numbers and organisation. At the moment we are safe, we have food, water and weapons and our building cannot be penetrated by the aliens. We will continue to broadcast on this frequency for another seven days, after which we will move to another location in an attempt to create a

colony of human survivors.'

'Who's that?' asked Georgia as she lifted her head from the kitchen table behind Steven.

'I found it as I was tuning the radio,' he replied, part of him feeling uncomfortable as he thought he recognised the voice that was being broadcast. 'It sounds like the whole country has been under attack from these creatures during the night. A group of survivors is in London trying to bring people together.'

'We are planning to send out regular scouting parties to find more survivors within the boundaries of London. If anyone hears this broadcast please make your way to the American Embassy in Grosvenor Square, London. We intend to fight back and create a secure area of the country to live in.'

'At least we know we're not alone,' said Tracker from the armchair. 'If we're to survive we had better make our way to London. Like the man on the radio said, there is safety in numbers and I certainly don't intend to stay here and wait to be eaten by one of the creatures. Let's pack up as much food and weapons as possible and plan a road trip to London.'

'The human race needs you. It must survive at any cost...'

If you are wondering what happens after Edgar and the children go through the portal, you will be pleased to know that the second Moon Stealer book is due for release later in 2012.

Look out for

The Moon Stealers and The Queen of the Underworld

Printed in Great Britain
by Amazon.co.uk, Ltd.,
Marston Gate.